GABRIEL DUMONT IN PARIS

GABRIEL DUMONT

JORDAN ZINOVICH

IN
PARIS

A NOVEL HISTORY

The University of Alberta Press

Published by
The University of Alberta Press
Ring House 2
Edmonton, Alberta T6G 2E2

Copyright © Jordan Zinovich 1999
ISBN 0–88864–321–7
Printed in Canada   5   4   3   2   1

A volume in (cuRRents), an interdisciplinary series. Jonathan Hart, series editor.

CANADIAN CATALOGUING IN PUBLICATION DATA

Zinovich, Jordan, 1955–
     Gabriel Dumont in Paris

     ISBN 0–88864–321–7

     1. Dumont, Gabriel, 1837–1906—Fiction. I. Title.
PS8599.I57G32 1998   C813'.54   C98–910804–X
PR9199.3.Z555G32 1998

Sketch of Gabriel Dumont courtesy of the Glenbow Archives, Calgary, Canada,
NA–2483–10. Photograph of Gabriel Dumont courtesy of the Glenbow Archives, Calgary,
Canada, NA–1177–1.

∞ Printed on acid-free paper.
Printed and bound in Canada by Friesens, Altona, Manitoba.

The University of Alberta Press acknowledges the financial support of the Government of
Canada through the Book Publishing Industry Development Program for its publishing
activities. The Press also gratefully acknowledges the support received for its program
from the Canada Council for the Arts.

The Canada Council | Le Conseil des Arts
FOR THE ARTS | DU CANADA
SINCE 1957 | DEPUIS 1957

Canadä

For George Zinovich, LC, and MO, all of whom pointed poetry at me.

ACKNOWLEDGEMENTS

I DOUBT VERY MUCH that I will be able to remember everyone who helped me during the course of my work on this project, so if your name does not appear here, my apologies. That said, I am very grateful to the following people, who were there for me at all times, but especially when I needed them most. Carole Beaulieu has been a steadfast collaborator on more than one project—I look forward to our next effort. Deb Creighton, Jim Feast, Jim Fleming, Harold Haft, Sharon Mesmer, Dana Rothkop, Rami Rothkop, and Peter Lamborn Wilson all read early versions of the manuscript and had insightful things to say. Glenn Rollans and Leslie Vermeer came through in unexpected and remarkably creative ways, and the final look and feel of this book is in large part a result of their suggestions and input. Martha Houle worked to add subtlety to the French. George Zinovich helped proof the final pages. And finally, Adele Haft is such a big part of everything I manage to accomplish that a mere thank-you never seems enough.

My breath explodes,
consuming naked trees.
Above the coughing rifles
Riel is bellowing:
Fight on my brave Métis.
You are the chosen ones
in this New World.

Patrice pleads: Now Exovede.
If ever
there was a time for miracles,
this is it.

Beyond the fighters I see the untouched church—
the priests inside it,
safe as the meat in eggs,
have sold us to our enemies.

When I part the brush Riel cries:
Uncle Gabriel!
We are beaten. What now?

"But Louis, you must always have known that we would be beaten. We are
defeated, so now we perish. Now they destroy us. Now you teach me the
lessons I must take from this."

PROLOGUE

History is a drowning pool of information. Facts? Facts are not isolated truths. They flow into and through one another. They cascade like the freshets of a waterfall echoing among cliffs. They are droplets striking the surface of history, absorbed so immediately that only spreading concentric ripples mark their entry. Guided by the ripples, historians struggle vainly toward the springs of origin and Truth. We wade and dive and twist and grope for the unrecoverable.

Everything I find and hear and see—each wave of voices, documents, and stories—flows into my ears and percolates through my mind. Intuition and integrity are beacons, but I have learned that only a mountebank would dare attempt to *assert* an absolute grasp of the ultimate foundations of Truth. The rain of facts branches into many streams of truth.

Who was Gabriel Dumont? I can not completely answer that for you—you must find the Truth of him yourself, if that is your concern. What happened to his people and culture? Again I say: search out your own answers. Much of the manuscript that follows is Gabriel's story as he himself told it to my friend M. Demanche. I have tried to organize Demanche's version and have added what research materials I could find to span its gaps. I tender this version only as a cautionary tale. Here are a leader and his troubled times.

We must start the story by posing a question: Do all our plans and best intentions decide any *real* aspects of our lives?

A. TRÉMAUDAN,
Montréal,
31 December 1899

I

my brothers Isidore and Edouard
my cousin Augustin and me,
small boys at Quill Lakes;
shivering aspens scatter
gold at our feet,
and in the hard blue sky
a trumpeting
flock of snow geese.
"I bet we can count them."
But they fly over us forever.

Dear Trémaudan:

I had heard that a Mister Riboulet worked with my friend
Gabriel Dumont on his memoir while Gabriel was in Staten
Island with Buffalo Bill's Wild West Show, but thought it only
a rumour. It was a project that I had always planned to under-
take myself. Now, learning that you have an almost complete
manuscript from this M. Demanche, of Paris, I am overwhelmed. For my part, I will of course assist you in any way I
can towards preparing it for publication. To that end I have
enclosed all the clippings, interviews, and letters I have saved
and gathered over the years since I lived with Gabriel—use
them as you see fit. I have also jotted down the most cogent of
my own memories. My hope is that this material of mine will
prove of value to your study of the old rebel.

Gabriel was about thirty-four years of age when I first met
him in 1872, but I initially believed him to be much older
because of his appearance. He is of medium height, square of
shoulder, with a homely but kind face and his chin adorned
with a scraggly beard. He is by no means huge, as many writers
have depicted him, and could not at that time have weighed

more than 165 or 170 pounds. His father, *Ai-caw-pow*, and his uncle, *Ska-kas-ta-ow* (these are phonetic renderings from the Cree), were, however, over six feet in height and heavily built. Even Louis Riel was taller than Gabriel.

Nor is Gabriel an ignorant savage, as certain writers assert. Far from it. He knows French and many different Indian dialects, and speaks Cree (his mother's tongue) with great facility. He has a remarkable memory, and can read and write both French and the Cree syllabics—as can his brothers Eli and Edouard. Edouard can also read music. Gabriel's wife, Madeleine, was a school teacher who read and wrote not only French and Cree, but fluent English as well.

And the man Gabriel—what of him? Which incidents speak most eloquently to me of his character?

First, in my experience he was kindly, and thoughtful of his Métis friends not endowed with worldly goods—although even he himself did not have much. I have seen him in one day kill eight buffalo and give them all to those in need.

He is a man of unquestioned courage whose word is heeded at the council above that of all others, even those many years his senior. His courage is the one point on which both his friends and enemies can agree.

When Gabriel speaks about his feats of arms, his lower jaw disengages and his mouth opens with a violent contraction. His dark eyes burn and a voice emerges like lightning, like the sounds of thunder rolling over armies on vast plains, like a great barrel rolling across an enormous echoing chamber. Then everything about him becomes huge—his feelings and heart, physique and intelligence; his mere presence.

At the early age of twenty-five, he became chief of the western buffalo hunt. It was Gabriel who enforced the "Law of the Plains," as the rules of the hunt were called. I once saw some young Indian boys ride into a large herd of buffalo just to lash the brutes. I remember vividly how Gabriel disciplined them, and the vengeance he threatened if they ever repeated their conduct.

He was always kind to me. His band always called me *le petit Canada*, but to the Dumont family themselves I was *cousin*, *neveu*, and to Gabriel always *mon frère*.

It was Gabriel whose steady nerves undertook whatever surgery the plains demanded. For example, the Indians could often get only a very inferior brand of gun, and one day we were running buffalo when one of the Crees with us had his gun explode, virtually tearing off his fingers. Gabriel examined the hand and told the Indian that the fingers had to come off. With a couple of swift strokes of Gabriel's skinning knife the job was done, and I heard that the wounds healed cleanly.

Need I say that he is a crack shot? I have never seen anyone quicker with a fowling piece than he is with the rifle. I completely understand how formidable he would be in a skirmish: to show an ear or an eye would mean being hit. I myself saw him put a bullet right through the head of a duck as it paddled near the rushes in a little lake, at a distance of not less than one hundred yards—which is by any account a remarkable shot. He said to me, "*Mon frère*, I'll take the head off that duck." And he did.

I remember another occasion when our camp was without meat for days. Captain after captain scouted the prairies for buffalo with no success. Gabriel then tried his powers. He started early in the morning; returned at noon with an antelope slung across his saddle and ordered us to strike camp; and that night we were camped beside *la foule*, as the hunters called the main herd.

He was also able to employ a queer trick mentioned by older generations of plains hunters: he could call the buffalo. It is a most impressive sight and once resulted in a dozen or so of the animals coming close enough for us to kill them.

Unfortunately, that hunt was in hilly country and the horse I had was a slewfoot. I was fortunate to come out alive.

Like any man, Gabriel has his faults. When in his cups he is given a wide berth by those who know him. Tales of his violence when double-crossed are fearsome indeed, and he is an inveterate gambler. I have known him to game for three days on end, stopping only to eat. But when fortune goes against him—and that is quite often—he is a good loser.

So, let me sum up the character of this old friend of mine. Gabriel Dumont is intelligent, courteous, kind, courageous, an A-1 hunter with an extraordinary knowledge of plains lore and the habits of the buffalo. He is ingenious, and is a man of strong likes and dislikes, but in no sense the bloodthirsty wretch that many of his enemies have painted him as being. Taken as a whole, he is a man to tie to. Among the councillors in any camp, when things got tight all the Métis turned to Gabriel.

Yours sincerely,

JOHN KERR

You want to know what life was like for me and my family? I will start with the first battle I was in. It was July 1851, on the Grand Coteau in mid summer—thick, golden grass glowing against orange buttes and dry grey coulees. Devil's Lake hunting ground lay before us. Days were very dry, and though some mornings mist shrouded our camp, the evening sun always set in fire. The Sioux were nearby. I was thirteen years old, with my little gun riding on my arm.

Nights, when we sometimes camped near a pond or swamp, a muttering crept through the darkness toward us. Big Baptiste Malterre told the little ones it was the sound of the poisonous plant that talks to itself. "He has two long roots like the legs of a man," joked Baptiste. "And beware, he only calms down when humans walk near. Then he starts hunting you!"

The Sioux had sworn that they would drive all us Métis hunters off the plains. Our caravan was only sixty-seven armed men and ten boys with rifles, with two hundred women and children trusting to our strength. The Red River hunters travelled one day's journey south of us. Two weeks out of Pembina, our scouts crested a ridge and observed Sioux tipis staining the distant prairie.

"Encircle the carts! *Vite! Vite! Animaux à l'intérieur.*" The shouts came from all sides.

We locked the carts together by jamming poles through the wheels, then heaped baggage under them to thicken our defensive wall. The women and children dug their trenches behind the carts. Isidore and I hurried to join the men, hollowing our rifle pit in the ring they made about sixty paces outside the carts. Once I glanced up from my hard work and saw Big Baptiste and three other hunters start off to scout the Indian camp.

"Gabriel!" called my father. "Take cover there, behind the carts."

"No," I said. "Isidore and me, we will fight from here." So he permitted me to stay, making certain that I had plenty of ammunition. My cousin Augustin was in a pit to the left of Isidore and me.

As night fell we heard the thunder of a galloping horse. Only one of our scouts returns—Baptiste and the others have been captured. The scout tells my father that there are five hundred Sioux lodges, thousands of warriors. Our leaders immediately send two men off to bring the River Red hunters to our rescue.

Stars leap out to spangle the clear night sky. A shadow swallows the swelling moon. An eclipse. The first I ever saw. "Gabriel," Isidore whispers from the darkness next to me. "Crawl back and get something to raise the front of our rifle pit."

I feel hungry, so I find some sacks of dried buffalo meat. "Gabriel," my mother says as I crawl off, "don't forget water. Take some for your father, too."

Back in the pit I say, "Isidore, we can eat these ramparts."

Dawn breaks slowly, in scarlet. Now I am afraid. Insects buzz in the rank grass near my nose. "Steady," says Isidore as a gang of warriors appears on the crest of the rise before us. More warriors appear until the prairie bristles with them, each one painted and half naked. They move slowly aside and a fierce-looking man strides to the front. He is unarmed, swinging a long rattle in one hand. He pauses, and a few riders split off from the main bunch.

Our ring of carts opens and my father and twenty or thirty other men ride out to parley. As the two groups approach each other I hear screaming and some shots. A lone rider breaks free of the Indians and gallops toward us. It is Jerome Magdalis, and he is terrified. "Don't permit them to reach the carts," he shouts as he passes. "They don't intend to let us go."

Isidore gives me a poke with his elbow and points. Big Baptiste sits on horseback surrounded by Indians.

The fierce Sioux is White Horse, a famous warrior. My father offers him gifts; says we only want to feed our families; asks leave to go. "Wagon men," says White Horse, "if you don't give us what we want, we will kill you all." He signals and more of his warriors leave the main bunch. Our hunters yank their horses around. The Indians try to cut them off, but they manage to reach our fortifications.

Behind me I hear the droning voice of our priest calling on God to help us. "Isidore! Gabriel!" my father calls when he returns to his rifle pit. "We must fight. Pick your shots with care. If they break through, try to reach the carts."

With a whoop, a young warrior charges against us. Isidore shoots him dead. *Le Petit* shakes in my hands. The Sioux charge.

We open fire and several other warriors fall. In the confusion Big Baptiste and our other scout try to break free. The horse of the other man is good and he makes it, but Big Baptiste falls to the earth. His body disappears in a pack of warriors, head and hands reappearing on the points of their spears—the battle has begun, and they will not show us mercy.

After their first charge, the Sioux fought more deliberately. They surrounded us, skirmished to find holes in our defenses. There were none. They tried to creep toward us. We kept them back. The sun rose higher and grew hot. Isidore and I chewed dried meat. We sipped our water. During the heat of day the Sioux tried another charge. More of them fell to our rifles, some twisting for a long time before growing still. My father was injured slightly, but only Big Baptiste was killed—his head staring down from a battle lance planted on the ridgetop, the flies crowding his grimace.

Late in the afternoon it grew quiet and a thunderstorm rolled over us. When it passed the Sioux were gone. The priest sent a group of us to bury Big Baptiste. We found all of him but the little finger from his left hand. His testicles were stuffed in his mouth, penis hanging out like a tongue.

This night I didn't sleep. Next morning we tried to retreat south. About an hour after we started, the Sioux were on us again. Again we drew the carts in a circle and dug our rifle pits.

We fought five hours more, until thunderclouds reared above us again. Then *les sauvages* charged in a group, swept around in single file, and fired one last volley.

We had won. That was my first real battle.

Everything I hear crawls in my ears and twists in my mind.
Trust comes slow as spring. As I grasped the world,
it seized me.

Madeleine Wilkie and I knew each other since we were children. We always liked one another, but didn't become friends until I was eleven and she about nine. This summer her father led the Red River hunters south, and my family went along with their Grand Caravan. We camped on the shores of Devil's Lake, and after dark the mutters began. The old people spoke about the evil plant, until finally I got curious. So I took *le Petit* and a torch and went hunting.

At first the sound seemed to come from near the lake. I crawled forward, and soon it was all around me. Then it stopped, suddenly. A noise in the bushes. I held the torchlight high, training *le Petit*'s muzzle ahead. Two red eyes stared hard at me, then disappeared. I was afraid. I don't know why I didn't fire, but instead I crawled on and discovered that the devil plant wore a dress.

"Hsst," whispered Madeleine. "*Regarde!* They are only small." She held a tiny muttering frog in the palm of her hand.

After that we spent a lot of time together.

Le Petit is my rifle. In 1848 my father learned that Louis Riel's father was organizing the Winnipeg Métis to oppose the Hudson's Bay Company. He and my uncles decided to journey to Fort Garry to see for themselves. They packed us into the carts, and off we went. I was about ten years old.

It was late spring. The water in the rivers was very high. Mud lay deep on the trail. We passed the Touchwood Hills and camped one night in a stand of trees beside a slough. That spring *les moustiques* were vicious, stinging until we bled. Every evening my father sent Isidore and me upwind to build smudge fires so our animals could take refuge in the smoke. This night we were gathering wood for our fires when I heard the sound of hooves.

Quick as a flash, Isidore and I raced back to the carts. "Papa," I shouted. "The Sioux are coming. Give me a gun to fight them."

"Where are they?" my father asked. We pointed.

Out went the cooking fires, and my father slipped into the night. In a few minutes he was back, smiling.

"Gabriel is too eager to fight," he laughed. "It is the buffalo that are coming, and here in these woods we are safe from them."

I was embarrassed and tried to sneak away, but Petit Cayen grabbed my shirt and dragged me into the flaring firelight. Petit was a bear—I could not move or shake him off. "So," he said. "You want a gun to fight the Sioux, eh? Isidore, *l'owasis ce n'est pas un poltron*, your boy is no coward."

Then my uncle Alex stood up. "Let him be, Petit," he said. "Gabriel, I'll give you the gun you want." He handed me a small musket that he used for bird hunting and said: "Learn quick, so you can help us when we really have to fight."

I called it *le Petit*, my little gun, which is what I've called all my rifles since.

That stand against the Hudson's Bay Company took place immediately before the spring hunts in 1849. My father and uncles rode in from White Horse Plain with all the other buffalo hunters. Everyone dressed in his best clothes; every hunter carried his favourite rifle. They went prepared to fight and die, and when Louis Riel's father came outdoors and said that we had beaten them, the shout went high: "*Le commerce est libre! Vive la liberté!*" And the rifles began a joyous fusillade.

The first winter he lived on his own, my cousin Augustin constructed a small cabin near the river. It had two comfortable rooms and he used green poplar wood for the rafters and roofing. It was near Christmas when he moved in. After one week of hot fires, the wood began to bud. On Christmas Day Madeleine and I were his guests, and he laughed at our surprise. His whole ceiling was in full green leaf.

Le Petit Amant
When I was very little, I was not very tall,
Hey when I was little, I was not very tall,
At ten years old, I chased the ladies all.
    Hia ha ha—that won't do!
    Hia ha ha—that won't do!
At ten years old, I hugged the ladies all,
When I was just ten, I loved the ladies all,
Sat in their laps to kiss them, I was so very small.
    Hia ha ha—that won't do!
    Hia ha ha—that won't do!

In their laps I kissed them, I was so very small,
Climbed in their laps to kiss them, I was so very small.
My mother came a running, shouting out her rage.

    Hia ha ha—that won't do!

    Hia ha ha—that won't do!

My mother came a running, screaming in a rage,
My mother came a running, shouting out her rage.
Go home, you little rascal, until you earn that wage.

    Hia ha ha—that won't do!

    Hia ha ha—that won't do!

Get home, you little rascal, until you earn that wage.
Stay home, you little rascal, you haven't earned that wage.
You can love the girls, my lad, when you come of age.

    Hia ha ha—that won't do!

    Hia ha ha—that won't do!

Wait to love the girls, my boy, until you reach that stage.
Ladies will be waiting, when you come of age.
So now I work at growing, but it's still so very small.

    Hia ha ha—it just won't do at all!

This is one of the songs that Madeleine loved.

JOHN KERR, *friend*

Gabriel really was very homely. With his scraggly beard he looked like a strange mix of beast and man. Madeleine, on the other hand, was very beautiful—wolf-willow slim with a fine full figure; comely; long black hair, honey-coloured eyes, a musical voice (she loved to sing), and movements as graceful as a soaring bird. I am almost ashamed to say that sometimes just looking at her made my mouth go dry. Much as I admired and liked Gabriel, I sometimes wondered what she saw in him.

LOUIS MARION, *plainsman*

All young men are heedless, but Gabriel was a lunatic.

One time we were out on the hunt when Philip Gariépuy rode over to our fire to tell us that he had stumbled onto a Blackfoot camp.

For a while Gabriel stays quiet. Then he says, "I feel like visiting. Anyone interested in coming along?"

See the scar here on my face? A Blackfoot warrior gave it to me, and this one on my arm too. At this time Gabriel was about twenty, and Alexi Lamerande and I were not going to permit him to boast. Not going to let him march off into the dark and return to tell us lies, either.

"Gabriel," I say, "if you want to give away your hair, I will be there to watch."

Then Alexi's low sweet voice says, "I will also come. But I don't want to fight, eh."

Neither of us know what Gabriel has in his mind—we go more out of curiosity than anything else. We ride out, each of us on a good horse, and find that Blackfoot camp hidden in a coulee. It was not big, maybe four or five tents—just enough fighters to make things hot if they discover us. We hobble our horses some way off, then crawl on our bellies until we feel the heat of their fire.

I am not ashamed to say that I was nervous. Gabriel had a Sarcee grandmother and I speak Blackfoot, so we understood that they were bragging. A big kettle boiled on the fire; drums throbbed; warriors danced and chanted, shaking trophy scalps and spearing pieces of meat from the kettle as they screamed the names of the Crees they had killed.

When I see Gabriel dancing toward their pot, the scent of blood fills my nostrils. "Me, I am Gabriel Dumont," he bellows, shaking le Petit in the air. "I have killed a lot of Blackfoot warriors, and I am hungry too."

The shocked air falls silent. Alexi looks over at me, his finger white on the trigger of his rifle. "*Merde!*" I think, "First I shoot that bastard Gabriel." But then their fiercest warrior explodes in laughter. "Brave man," he says, "sit here and smoke with me. Eat with us."

I always stayed on good terms with the Crees, and one time Madeleine and I camped with a bunch of them. One day when I was away, a warrior came to our tent and asked Madeleine to give him a good buffalo pony that I had left hobbled with a chain. She said, "No!" So the Cree said, "If you don't open the lock, I will kill the horse." So Madeleine gave him the horse.

When I returned and found this out, I went cold. This same night the Crees had a war dance because they were planning to fight the Blackfoot. I slipped into the lodge and sat down quietly among the women. When it was near morning and the warriors had finished dancing, I jumped up and demanded to speak.

"Friends, I have hunted buffalo with you and fought your enemies," I said, "and today you insult me. I was not there when you took my horse. It was not brave to scare my wife. Since we were married we have always been together and I have protected her, and when you do something to her you do it to me. I warn you now: I will not let this pass."

They said that they had not meant to offend me, but their law obliged their allies to supply their best horses to the warriors going to fight.

"I do not follow your laws," I said, "but I will fight beside you here and now. I will demonstrate my courage. Not one of you will charge ahead of me into battle, and when I finish with your enemies and they fear me, you will know that I am not a liar. If things go any other way you can take my horse. But as long as I am first into battle, I demand that you respect my wife and leave my property alone when I am not there."

That morning we fought the Blackfoot. One of their young warriors was more daring than the rest. He came toward us alone and I rode furiously toward him. He fled. I hunted him as I would hunt a buffalo. When I caught him, I planted the barrel of my rifle against his heart and fired. He fell on the neck of my horse and then slipped to the earth. My horse reared, nearly throwing me. The Blackfoot pony was next to me so I jumped down and caught its bridle. When I returned to the warrior, he had died, and a great sorrow took hold of me. He had never hurt me. I only killed him to humiliate the men who had insulted Madeleine.

Do you really think that I recall these battles to boast? Every one represents a struggle, and I tell you this: the Métis always fought for liberty. We only wanted the right to make decisions for ourselves, and to wander freely on our earth. If there had to be a Government that the Canadians would accept, we wanted some say in it. We asked to be heard, and deserved that much respect.

I am no coward, but your cities overwhelm me. Your politics is all words and unrealizable plans, and each one strikes me a blow. I hear the baying and recognize that none of your orators could survive a winter night on the prairies, or an encounter with a clever enemy intent on killing them. They convince me that they know nothing of thirst or loss, weakness or doubt. They will never actually experience an idea's bloody afterbirth. What do they understand about the lives we led or the crises we faced? I ask only for money and support. Find an unscarred boy to offer the good ideas to.

We experienced many bizarre things out on the prairie. One night in mid winter, my family was moving along the frozen Qu'Appelle River toward Fort Ellice. Isidore tramped ahead, breaking the track. The snow hissed under our sleighs. The moon shone low in the sky and ice stuck to my eyebrows and beard. My snow-heavy moccasins sparkled with tiny pale rainbows every time I raised a foot. And suddenly we seemed to be walking on the moon. Each shadow stood sharp-cut from the night. The northern lights twisted in fire and blue flames flared around each one of us. Every hair on my head stood up. The dogs howled, their coats bristling. The hair on the buffalo robes stiffened like the quills on a porcupine. Then the blue flames stopped. No one was harmed, no one burned.

That was the year of the smallpox, the year my mother died. It was the year Madeleine became my wife and we moved out on our own. Soon families would walk in circles to avoid each other, and the stinking, unburied dead rotted under the dancing sky.

My mother did not die of the smallpox—it was something else, but the smallpox is what I remember. The smallpox and the cold blue fire. And Madeleine.

Father, give me courage, and belief, and faith in the holy blessing I have received in Your holy name, so that I will remember this event up until the hour of my death. Amen.

Isidore was nineteen, I was fifteen, and Edouard and Elie were small boys when, one afternoon in the spring, we decided to go hunting. Without asking my father for permission, we followed the Saskatchewan south from the forks, then struck out into the wind and deep prairie. By the end of the first day we were past the Minichinas Hills. By the second we were alone in enemy territory, with nothing to stop the Sioux or Blackfoot from lifting our hair.

Hunting was good. The air was still or blew toward us. Cabree came up to us without fear. Rabbits and prairie chickens stumbled into our snares. One shot and anything we aimed at fell. Isidore kept Edouard and Elie next to him, teaching them to follow tracks and hunt. Every morning I set off alone to keep the watch.

One warm evening we camped at a narrows on the upper Qu'Appelle River. Before the sun had set the moon began to swell, and we sat near our fire watching it grow mysterious and full, staring eastwards across the river bottom toward the coulees and prairies beyond. Not a breath of wind that evening. Slowly, a dark stain spread over the crests of the distant coulees. It hesitated, then a wave of blackness cascaded down toward us. First there was not a sound. Then came a rushing, faint like a wind stirring the leaves.

But it was not the wind. It was *la foule*, the great herd moving right toward where we were camped. A pure white cow led them, marching on in advance of the others, shining out in the clear moonlight. Four big bulls followed her, walking side by side, and then came a column of all ages, sizes, and descriptions spreading behind them as far as we could see. The ghost cow reached the riverbank and stopped, the herd fanning out behind her.

The wind we had heard was the sound of their breathing, fused now in a continuous roar. We held our breath and watched, not lifting our rifles. Still she hesitated. Thousands of buffalo had backed up behind her, and still the cascade flowed down from the prairie. Slowly she ambled forward to drink. When she was filled, she splashed toward us. Then all heads went high, and the others followed to take their turn.

The buffalo were water drunk when they reached our side of the river. They stumbled as they climbed up the riverbank, scattering to either side of our campfire. Onward without changing direction, a dark sea of drunken buffalo with us an island in its heart. Dawn was breaking when the last old bull and tottering calf swerved past us. They had almost drunk the river dry: I walked across it without getting my ankles wet.

Was anyone ever happier than the first buffalo hunter to ride a horse?
Space collapses—distant herds draw nearer. How he felt, uphill and down.
How he swept across the flat prairies. The sight of a bellowing dark sea.
Killing one, then another and another. The absolute joy of riding, the flow
of it under and through me.

My horse a vessel
breasting the spindrift
snow.
SMASH
the bugling wind;
bone white
bellyfat for the chickadees
—little enough to offer
friends.
Twenty years ago
les animaux
sustained us
and skies dawned
as wide as
—No! Wider than—
Government promises.

You and your politicians miss it, but there is one thing that everyone *must* realize: the Indians of North America own North America. Only by recognizing this and uniting with them in marriage can the white man ever make any real claim on the country. The Métis are brothers to the Indians by blood and share their right to the land.

NORBERT WELSH, *plainsman*

Speak all you want to about how noble and great Gabriel Dumont is. Speak about the trouble alcohol caused and the love Gabriel has for the Indians, but he was just like all the rest of us. All us Métis traded alcohol to the Indians. I myself didn't ever take trade goods and alcohol together, because when the Indians got drunk they wanted things for free. So on one trip I carried alcohol, and on the next one trade goods. In 1864 I brought two big kegs of alcohol from Fort Garry. But as I was trading, it came to me what bad deals I was making—selling such a lot of alcohol to the Indians. I decided to make the alcohol stronger; I diluted it one to two, instead of one to three. Ho! My Indians discovered the difference right away and wanted to know why. "The second barrel was stronger than the first," I said. "Oh! Oh! We understand," they said.

My idea was to get rid of the alcohol as quickly as possible. My conscience told me that I sold them too much water. I traded away all the alcohol, and my conscience was eased.

About the middle of April a big thaw came. All us fur traders packaged our fur and buffalo robes, and loaded our carts in preparation to starting for Fort Garry. We were a big company, about one hundred and fifty carts and thirty families. Before we left, we appointed a chief and four sub-officers to direct the trip. Our chief this time was Gabriel Dumont. It took us four days to journey from Round Plain to Devil's Lake. By then it had gotten cold again. We camped next to the big bush that was there then, and me and three other young fellows guarded the horses through the night.

The Indians always followed us when we left the prairie, to steal back the horses that they had traded for alcohol. We traders had some special laws of our own at those times. On this trip Dumont charged us to address every stranger in three languages—French, Cree, and Assiniboine—and if he didn't answer, to shoot him.

Oh, it was cold—blowing hard and freezing! I can feel the chill now. Each of us had a thick buffalo robe, but we could not sleep. I was lying on my stomach wrapped in my robe. A big horse fed near me. All at once he lifted his head and snorted. It was very dark. The horse snorted again, then jumped, and I made out a man crouched down, crawling on all fours like a wolf.

I put my gun aside and crawled toward him. When the thief bent to undo the hobble, I leaped on his back, wrapping my arms around his body. He was terrified. He was a big, big man and I was only a moderately sized young fellow. He nearly threw me off, but my comrades heard me shouting and came to help me. We took our prisoner to Dumont's tent.

Gabriel tied the man up and kept him for the night. The next morning he called us to his tent and asked who had first laid hands on the prisoner. The boys said it was me, and Dumont told the prisoner that he was lucky I had not followed orders. He said that I was a terrible man, afraid of nothing, and that if he tried to steal our horses again, I would horsewhip him—there is nothing an Indian fears more than the humiliation of a whipping. Then Gabriel gave him some tea, sugar, and tobacco and sent him back to tell his gang never again to try stealing horses from the camp of a Dumont.

Life strung bowstring taut; Every sound a signal;
Every rustle is death.
Whispers in my mind,
until I can not think or sleep or shit for fear.
Will they capture me?
Does screaming ease the pain?
I say: "To hell with this! None of us get out of life alive.
Why stay here crapping my trousers?
Act now, and die."

Life was always exciting out on the prairie. One day I am scouting for buffalo. I hobble my horse and climb a kind of double-top butte. I am not completely to the top when I see something hidden among some rocks on the other hill. I slip in low, face first, and work my way around. I think to myself, "It is either a wolf or a man lying on his side." If I howl, a man will freeze and listen but a wolf will run. I watch a while then cry out. He was a man. He seemed to listen for a long time. After a time I begin to think that he must be asleep, but I must know for certain. I decide to go and visit him. I crawl back and ride my horse around to the base of the hill where the man slept.

If I had tried to ride near him, he might have gotten the jump on me, so I leave my horse at the bottom of the hill. As I crawl near, I see that he is asleep with his rifle on the earth next to him. If I waken him, he will be afraid and go for his gun to shoot me. I have le Petit in my hand, ready to fire. I creep nearer, calm like a wolf, and silently take away his rifle, then fall back and put it on the earth behind me.

Now there is no danger, so I decide to wake him up. He is a Gros Ventre. He has a full head of matted hair and a big strong body. He is my enemy, so I take the rawhide whip I carried and whip the air above him. Suddenly he is on his knees, a terrified look on his face. And I can not help myself: I begin laughing. I laugh so hard that he begins laughing, too.

Still laughing, I sat down next to him. Keeping my rifle far away from him, I found my pipe and lit it. The Indian took it with pleasure and smoked deeply. Then his whole body began to tremble so violently that he could not hold the pipe. He showed me by signs how much I had frightened him.

Finally we rose. I gave him back his rifle. But when we reached my horse, which was still hobbled, I realized that I would have to bend to free its legs. An Indian warrior who has been humiliated can be vengeful. I was afraid to untie my horse, afraid the Gros Ventre would shoot me as I bent over. So I sign to him that he must go down to his horse at the bottom of the hill. He goes and rides off at top speed, like a devil is after him.

Many years later, when I made peace between our nations, I met my old prisoner in a Gros Ventre camp. It was twenty years since our first meeting, and though he had white hairs among his dark locks I recognized him. He was Bull's Hide, a great chief of his nation. We laughed and smoked together again.

During the summer evenings on the prairie in my childhood, the scouts set off to watch against attack even before the carts were unhitched. We watered our animals and every family started its fire. The women prepared whatever game we had killed during the day. Isidore would make the bannocks, which is what we called our bread—his always was the best. On the fire, a soup or rabbit or bird boiled.

After we ate, the men smoked and my brothers and I built the smudge fires to keep away the mosquitoes. Voices rose from every corner of the camp. At sunset a bell rang to call us to prayer. The priest waited for us in front of an altar heaped high with wild flowers honouring the heavenly Queen of Flowers, the Mother of God. Night had fallen by the end of the service, and the stars were out.

Every family returned and stirred its fire back to life. The old people began telling their histories and tales, and here and there a violin scraped up a song. You can not imagine the happy freedom of sleeping outdoors on the open prairie. Nature abounds with life. In the distance we heard the bellowing of the buffalo and the barking prairie dogs and foxes; from farther away came the yapping of the coyotes, and in the far distance the deep-howling wolves called back and forth from the tops of the hills. The thrumming moans of the nighthawks and the drumming prairie chickens and the whistling whippoorwills filled all the silent spaces.

We called 1862 the Year of the Great Peace. It was ten years after my first battle on the Grand Coteau when we fixed our treaty with the Sioux at Devil's Lake near Les Isles du Mort. The celebration lasted three days, and the Sioux declared that the country belonged as much to us as it did to them, and that the buffalo existed for us both.

I was twenty-four years old, just an observer. My father and uncle spoke for the Métis, but the negotiations were not simple. Who could forget Big Baptiste Malterre? There was deep anger and suspicion on both sides. One day I was leaving the tipi where I was staying, bending down through the narrow opening, when an angry warrior hit me over the head with his rifle and pulled the trigger. Fortunately the shot missed, but I still have a bruise here, above my hairline. The other warriors kicked the man. They beat him with sticks and drove him from the camp.

We all had too much at stake. The Americans were forcing the Minnesota Sioux towards war. The Lakota Sioux wanted the certainty that we would not strike at their backs, should they too have to fight. That was when I first began to think that all the peoples of the plains would soon have to ally against the eastern invaders.

The year after the celebrations at Devil's Lake my father married Angèle and moved to the Red River to start a new family. Then my uncle Jean moved south of the Saskatchewan to the Cypress Hills. When the hunters chose a captain for the 1863 hunting, I was the only Dumont left. I was twenty-five, and from 1863 until the buffalo disappeared I led the Saskatchewan hunt.

WILLIAM F. BUTLER, *traveller*

Autumn. Ten days dawn and die; the Mauvais Bois, the Spirit Sands—western shore of an ancient world's immense lake. The stretching hills of the Little Saskatchewan rise, draw near, and fade behind me. A wild storm from the north rages a day and a night, tearing off the yellow leaves and chasing the wild birds southward.

I travel through an unending vision of sky and grass— toward a dim, distant, ever-shifting horizon. Ridges roll one motionlessly upon another. Sunrise and sunset: night narrows to nothing and morning expands the same formless void. The sigh of a solitary breeze is the voice of this universe. Over everything towers the sense of empty, endless distance, which comes when day after day has dawned on the same grass and sky.

This view is so vast that it embodies space itself, and with a single glance I am fulfilled. No mountain rears against the skyline; no glistening river twists across the middle distance; no dark forest shades the foreground or fringes my perspective. Reduced to its own nakedness, space stands grandly forth, and I face that enigma that humans vainly try to reduce by calling it "infinite," "relentless," "boundless."

Your River Seine reminds me of our Saskatchewan. It has the same soft, fat, slick, brown skin with a greenish tinge. In summer, the stands of trees strike out like feathers from the hollows at its neck. I love to swim. I was five or six years old when my father dropped me into the clear lakes at Qu'Appelle. I remember sinking wide-eyed past his hairy white legs into the green weeds on the bottom. The surface was a looking glass. Bubbles raced upwards past me. My lungs were filled and swelling, and every sound was weak and far away like half-remembered music. When I bobbed back to the surface, he plucked me out and showed me how to float and move my arms.

Water is another world. I spent all the time we stayed at Qu'Appelle immersed in the lakes. I would rise slowly until my ears rested on the surface and I was suspended in the two worlds.

Madeleine loved those lakes, but the river was muddy and whispered. She would not swim in the river.

During the summer of 1863, it grew very hot. Madeleine could not sleep. For weeks all she thinks of, all she will speak of, is that we don't have children. At first I think it is the heat, but after a time I begin to worry. She chats, then falls restlessly silent for days. She wonders out loud how we have offended God. Travelling is the only thing that helps to calm her.

We visit Isidore at Round Prairie, then Elie, then Edouard at Old Wives Lake. I can not reach her. She is lost to me. We stop a time with Augustin, then with Madeleine's sisters by the cool blue lakes at Qu'Appelle. Augustin makes her smile, but nothing else reaches her. I try more water—Crooked Lake, Round Lake, Birdtail River, the Assiniboine. If nothing works, maybe we will have to visit the priests at Saint François Xavier.

After one complete change of the moon I have an idea. As the sun sets I turn us north from the Assiniboine, away from Saint François. In a few hours we reach le Mauvais Bois, the Spirit Sands. We roll deep into the dunes as a wind rises and the sand begins to hiss. Soon there is nothing but the hiss of white sands and some dark whispering spruce trees. A moon with a big bite out of it. Everything is gleaming light: white like winter, white like snow. Madeleine grows silent. Her eyes change. Her forehead smoothes.

Suddenly she laughs. "Remember that Christmas in Augustin's cabin?" she asks.

Some months later we adopted Annie, and my nephew Alexi became like a son to me.

COLONEL CROFTON, *to the British War Office*

Should it ever be necessary to raise an irregular cavalry in the Canadian West, there exists in the half-breeds of the North West Territories the most eligible material I have ever seen in any country, and I have seen the Risalus of India and the Bedouin Arabs. The half-breeds are a splendidly organized society when on the prairies, and the combination of their superb knowledge of the country and their ability to live off it when necessary would render them a very formidable enemy if they ever rebelled against the constituted authorities.

On a second hunt during the winter of 1865, I led twenty or thirty men across the river. For two days we didn't see any sign of buffalo. Our rations were getting low, so I called a meeting and the hunters asked me to suggest a plan.

I chose three scouts: one to go southeast, another southwest, the third northwest.

I went northeast. Norbert Welsh, who was the youngest but not the least boastful, went southwest, toward where Calgary is now. That was the most dangerous ground, the Blackfoot country. I told him to go as far as the forks of the Red Deer and Saskatchewan rivers. There he would find a big hill where he could safely get a good wide view of the country. Baptiste Parenteau went southeast; he also had a hill to climb. Joseph Azure went northwest.

I did not see any signs of *les animaux*, and neither did Parenteau or Azure. Welsh was the last one back, and he had a story to tell.

He said that he had let his big horse gallop until he had reached the hill and climbed to the top. The sun told him that it was time to eat, so he ate his meal there, letting his horse drift to the end of its tether. All at once it jumped and whinnied. The hairs on its shoulders stood up.

When a hunter scouts alone, he tries never to go back the way he came, especially if he climbs a hill. If your enemies see you, they will wait at the foot of the hill to capture you as you descend. Welsh was watching a ravine that runs back to the river when something shone across his eyes. In the glare he could just make out what looked like deer, so he started down in that direction. At the foot of the hill, he whipped his horse on but it reared. He gave it another lash. It bounded and reared again, so he decided to let his horse have its head, and on his way back toward the camp, in the distance he saw an old buffalo facing the wind and pawing at the snow.

I told everyone that before noon next day we would be overrun with buffalo. Then I told Welsh that he was lucky that he had a good horse or the Blackfoot would have gotten him. They were disguised as deer and had shone a looking glass across his eyes to lure him on.

When we rose next morning there were buffalo everywhere. On our second day in that camp, a Cree galloped in demanding cartridges. He said that near the ravine where Welsh had seen the deer, Pierre Quinzanse and his wife had been skinning a buffalo. The Blackfoot had killed them. They opened their bodies and drank the blood from their hearts.

I remember only one time that we enforced the harshest Prairie Law. The whole Deschamps family was bad. They broke every camp rule: stole, seduced young girls. Finally, one of them even attacked a member of the hunt council when we ruled against him. So one night they went to bed, and someone cut their throats quietly in the dark. We buried them where they lay, marking their graves so that every time Métis travellers passed the place they would remember the judgement against the Deschamps.

JOHN KERR, *plainsman*

In October, the buffalo herds began a slow march toward the wooded country near the foothills of the Rockies. It was a sight to see a drove of thousands of majestic animals moving a

few steps, then pausing for a mouthful of grass; always travelling in one direction. When spring came the following year,
they would turn and make again for the open prairie.

It took very little to set a whole herd on the stampede,
turning the landscape, in the twinkling of an eye, into an
undulating sea of backs. The noise of hoofs cracking and horns
clashing would soon be lost in a thunderous pounding of feet.
In the summer months, the sound was a hollow rumble; in
the fall, when the ground was frozen, it was a more clattering
staccato. Woe to any living thing in the path of a stampeding
herd of buffaloes. Darkness increased the strange panics that
possessed them. On they would go, lunging and plunging, till,
through sheer exhaustion they came to a halt, panting,
tongues lolling out, flanks heaving, eyes wild and bloodshot.

FRANCIS DICKENS, *policeman*

The buffalo is a pitifully vulnerable beast, peculiarly
Canadian in being very sociable yet somewhat near-sighted, as
subject as a cat to fatal curiosity but without the compensation of having nine lives.

Life on the prairie can be hard, and every hunter
knows enough to try never to let meat go to waste, especially
during the winter. In March of 1866 there was a blizzard that
lasted three days. Three miles from my camp a big herd of
buffalo tried to cross the Saskatchewan River, fell through the
ice, and was frozen in. There must have been a thousand
animals frozen in the ice. I walked from one bank of the river to

the other on their backs. Toward spring, when it began to melt, the Crees cut the carcasses out and saved the hides and meat.

We Métis chose our winter camps with care. They had to have wood for building materials and fuel, and be near a stream or river and not far distant from the buffalo. We returned to the good places.

By the early 1870s we could already see that the buffalo were disappearing, and my people wanted priests and schools for their children. Our first real settlement in the Saskatchewan was called La Petite Ville. It was on the west bank of the Saskatchewan, opposite Fish Creek. About the time that Father André arrived, the Hudson's Bay Company sold the North West Territories to Canada. We thought that was strange. We had not given the country to the Hudson's Bay Company. The Indians hadn't. How could they sell what they didn't own?

The slow transition of late fall into winter.
Snow is silent,
omnivorous, and as allegorical as bones.
It swallows sound as it swallows the prairie.
The first true winter sunrise is always a bleeding hole
in the dark side of the sky.

I first met Louis Riel in 1869, at Winnipeg. That first revolution had been nearly bloodless—the Métis nation had international law on its side. At first the Canadians agreed to our demands, but then they sent an army to "keep the peace." It was a lie! They planned to trap Riel and his council, to try them for killing that stupid man Scott. In June of 1870 I sent Riel a message that said: "*Si tu fais quelque chose, envoie-moi chercher, et je viendrai avec les sauvages.* Don't let that bastard English army enter our country. Send for me, and I will return with 500 wild fighters."

Voulez-vous écouter chanter
Une chanson de vérité?
Le dix-neuf de juin la bande des Bois-Brûlés
Sont arrivés comme des braves guerriers.

En arrivant à la Grenouillère
Nous avons pris trois prisonniers:
Trois prisonniers des Arkanys
Qui sont ici pour piller notre pays.

Etant sur la point de débarquer
Deux de nos gens se sont mis à crier:
Deux de nos gens se sont mis à crier:
Voilà l'Anglais qui vient nous attaquer!

Le Gouverneur qui se croit Empereur,
Il veut agir avec rigueur;
Le Gouverneur qui se croit Empereur
A son malheur, agit trop de rigueur.

Don't make so much of what a great chief Gabriel Dumont was. There are stories that I can tell, too. In July of 1871 I was with a brigade that started from Batoche, which was the only crossing on the south branch of the Saskatchewan River. By the time we reached Sounding Lake, we had found the buffalo. I ran two races and killed twelve. While we skinned the buffalo and dried the meat, Gabriel Dumont galloped into our camp and asked to see Charles Trottier, who was the chief of our brigade. We were the biggest group in the region so, as custom demanded, Dumont asked to join our camp. Trottier asked how many families were with him. He answered that there were two Métis families and about twenty-five families of Indians.

We had heard that this brigade of Dumont's had the smallpox. Trottier mentioned this and demanded to know why he had not said so. Dumont answered that he had not had the time to explain that the Métis families were not sick. After a discussion with everyone, Trottier agreed to permit Dumont and the two Métis families to join us in two or three days, if none of them developed the illness by then. However, until then they must camp at a distance.

Dumont was not a good chief, and I don't know how he got his reputation as one. He could not control his Indians. When the whole brigade arrived, we had to use our guns to keep them out of our camp. We kept them a half mile away from us, but they came at night and washed their sores in our springs.

The soil was very sandy and it was easy to find water, so we dug four new wells, one at each corner of our camp, and appointed four men to guard them. On the third day, just as we prepared to let the Métis families join our camp, a relative of Dumont's died of the smallpox: a sister's child. Because of this we could not let them join us. Once they had the illness there was nothing anyone could do for them.

It was the black smallpox. One day I visited their camp, and what a pathetic sight it was. I was on horseback. It was a hot summer, and the sick ones lay scattered all over. Horrible cramps drew their bodies up until they rested on the tips of their heels and the tops of their heads. Some days ten or twelve persons died in agony.

By this time we were well supplied with pemmican and dried meat. In order to shake Dumont's brigade, Trottier led us to Round Plain. After leaving us, Dumont went to the camp of his father, at Batoche, where they also had smallpox. When we reached our wintering place, a message came from Batoche asking us for alcohol. Alcohol was the only treatment we knew of for smallpox, and Dumont wanted ten gallons.

Trottier came to me and said that his house was not yet finished. My house was completed, so I agreed to make the trip to Batoche, a distance of sixty miles. It took four days to go there and back. The people at Batoche were very happy to see me. Some were better, but before I entered their camp I took a big glass of liquor, which was what the doctors recommended. It was getting cold and the illness was dying out. Dumont's sister-in-law had recovered but was covered with scabs that would not come off. Her husband took his pocket knife and cut off the ones on the soles of her feet.

We knew the buffalo were vanishing, but it was at the suggestion of Lawrence Clarke and Father André that we decided to "civilize" ourselves, and choose the site for our St. Laurent Colony. Our boundaries began at St. Louis in the north, ran south along both sides of the South Branch of the Saskatchewan River as far as my farm at Gabriel's Crossing, and extended six miles west to include the settlement at Duck Lake.

We surveyed traditional Métis lots, giving each farmer about two hundred yards along the river and the rights to as much land back from the river as he could see under the belly of a big horse, which was about two miles. He also had hay rights extending two miles farther into the prairie.

I kept up the alliances my father made with the Sioux in the Year of the Great Peace. And over the years as I travelled over the prairie trading and talking with other bands and Indian tribes, I gave gifts of tobacco and spoke about what we could do if the Englishmen tried to take over our country. Words bound by tobacco, they were a beginning.

One day some friends were eating with me in my tent when Big Bear rode into my camp. He and I had smoked together many times. We were friendly, but not friends. He was a great orator, and I invited him to eat with me.

There was only one large buffalo herd in Saskatchewan that spring, and we were hunting it. By Prairie Law, smaller bands of hunters had to join the largest camp to hunt the main herd. When Big Bear asked to hunt without joining our camp, I said, "Nemoia! No!" He stalked out of my tent.

This was 1873. We had a great big camp of Métis from St. Laurent, Fort Qu'Appelle, and Wood Mountain, as well as Crees from Fort Carlton and Fort Pitt. My uncle Jean had come up from the Cypress Hills to join us, and my father was back from the Red River. Our St. Laurent group was largest, equaling all the other Métis combined; the Crees had about forty lodges in all. A week or so after Big Bear joined us, we laid up for five days to cure robes, make pemmican and dry meat, and rest our horses.

But when we returned to the hunt most of the herd had vanished. My scouts told me there were small bands of buffalo within sight of our camp, but the main herd had been moved off. At a council meeting we discussed the situation. We sent Pierre Poitras to ask the Cree chiefs to join us, and three came.

"Where is Big Bear?" my uncle Jean asked. "Bring him!"

Big Bear entered with his shoulders humped up in defiance. My scouts repeated their discovery, and all the Cree chiefs denied having anything to do with it.

"Are all your young men in camp?" asked my uncle.

"Ah-huh, *tap-way*," answered three of them.

"How about your young men?" I asked Big Bear.

He shrugged. "My young men come and go as they please," he said.

"We are hunting here. Are you the chief? Or not?"

"Yes, but young men are wild."

"You're not much of a chief, then," I said.

"I am chief," began Big Bear, getting angrily to his feet.

I interrupted him: "*Oui*! I know your sort of chief. If any of your young men have played a part in this, you will pay."

My tall uncle and my father moved to stand beside me. Big Bear's glance grew unsteady. He turned and left the tent, followed by the other chiefs.

Then the council agreed that my cousin Petit Jean and I should try to draw the herd back. When John Kerr asked if he could come along, I said, "Let him come."

"But he has only a broken-down, skinny old mare," my cousin said.

"I will lend him a horse," I said, and the matter was settled.

We left shortly after noon of the next day, rode until our horses were tired, then topped a rise and came suddenly upon our buffalo. To the right lay the North Saskatchewan snaking in and out, marked by timber and brush along its banks. Thousands of *les animaux* quietly drank its muddy water. Thousands more slowly cropped the grass. Still more lay about in small groups or wallowed in the dust, and from a small slough a few hundred yards away, flocks of ducks burst up where more buffalo were wading and tossing their shaggy heads. There was nothing else in sight—nothing but the broad prairie.

"There they are," said Petit Jean. I nodded. My eyes took in the poplar trees shimmering in the setting sun; grunting buffalo slapped at flies with their short tails or scratched themselves against the trees while others dropped to their knees and rolled over to wallow, their great heads and shoulders raising little mounds of dust, their beards sweeping the grass. I saw nothing to startle them, yet they had been continuously on the move for four days.

"We have found the buffalo," I said. "But where are the Crees?"

"Over there," answered Petit Jean. He pointed, and sure enough there was a thin plume of smoke rising about a mile back from the opposite riverbank.

"The best thing we can do is to go down into the woods by the river and camp," I said. "We will get up early tomorrow and start them back."

"Look again," said Jean. "*Les sauvages* have pushed some across."

I made out animals moving across the river above the Indian encampment. "True," I said, "but not so many. If we try for those, *les cris* will cross and drive the whole herd over. No! We make camp and get an early start. Once we have the buffalo on the move, they will never stop them."

So we took our horses to drink, then hobbled them away from the river. As the darkness came on we built a fire, ate a little, then smoked. There wasn't a bright moon, but it was fairly light.

"What about the horses?" John Kerr asked.

"*Ça va, mon frère.* They'll be all right," I said.

"Well, I'll just go and check on them," he said.

Jean snickered: "*Vas-y, Petit Canada. Dépêche-toi mon brave!*"

Not too long afterward we heard a shout and rushed up to find Kerr wrestling with a young Cree. The warrior would not say a word, and Jean would not let me force him, so we took him prisoner. We brought our horses in and waited out the night near the fire.

Just before daybreak we watered the horses again and saddled up. Jean wanted to release the prisoner, but I refused—we rode off with my gun pointed at the young Cree's chest. As we neared the buffalo we yelled and fired into the air. Up and away they went, converging bunch by bunch until the whole herd was moving toward the open prairie.

We kept between them and the river and didn't hurry. About noon we rested for a few hours. Then after urging the herd on for another hour or so we headed for our camp, leaving the buffalo to wander on their own.

A crowd gathered at the council tent this night. I told my story and the meeting broke up. The next morning we learned that our prisoner was one of Big Bear's young men. He and five others had been sent to move part of the herd across the river toward Fort Pitt. Their luck had held for three days.

We discussed what to do with Big Bear. He refused to take responsibility for his young men. I reminded him that he himself had chosen them. He said he had told them to isolate only enough buffalo so his band would not have to cross the river to hunt. We argued back and forth until I grabbed a gun and jabbed him in the stomach with the butt of it. In the end we fined him a horse and a cart and sent his young men out to bring back the buffalo they had chased across the river.

Big Bear and I both wanted to unite the plains people. This was the first time we had disagreed in public, but I know that this incident is part of the reason that he did not help defend Batoche.

Nothing I say will help you imagine a buffalo; its vitality; the bellowing rut and wild stampedes and the rank odour of guts when we opened one up— the heat on my arm swimming elbow deep in blood; the peppery satisfying taste of hot raw liver dipped in bile; the sense of loss every time I sliced away a long white penis and laid it away in the dust. Every Métis child was born to this. How can you know our loss?

2

Riel said: "Priests are not religion. They are empowered to maintain the spirit of religion, but their authority exists only as long as they remain faithful to their mission. When they stray, as ours have, they lose their usefulness."

JOHN DONKIN, *policeman*

Father André is a stocky, broad shouldered, powerful Breton; an obstinate man, with no social graces but a huge heart and extraordinary zeal. He reminds me very much of those Greek Orthodox priests you often see in the dock areas of seaport towns. When I first met him he wore a lofty beaver hat, a filthy, threadbare cassock, and a long, unkempt, iron-grey beard. Whatever the Saskatchewan Métis did, he was prepared to do too. It did not take them long to accept him as their priest.

About the time that Father André settled himself at St. Laurent, Madeleine and I moved permanently to Gabriel's Crossing. Xavier Letendre, whom all Métis call Batoche, had built his store near St. Laurent and established a ferry across the river. But travellers going to and from Fort Carlton had to go out of their way to use it. So Madeleine and I settled farther south, on the direct route, and established a ferry of our own.

We built in a small meadow, on a point ringed by aspens and black poplars in a crook near the river's shoulder. We were near an easy hill down to the water with a long sandy beach at the bottom, and were as happy as children. "Let's build the house here; stable there; store there. And we'll have a big garden, too," we said. That was the only house we ever owned, a log house, weather-tight and trim with plastered walls, a plank floor, and a second storey. I painted the front of it bright blue and the other walls white, and Madeleine planted roses, yellow daisies, and day lilies on either side of the door.

One day my friend Damase Carrière rode up. "Priests!" he spat in disgust. "I have to get away. This new priest slaps us when he thinks he can get away with it. 'In the name of Christ,' he says. For *our* good. In God's name!"

"He would never strike me," I said.

"That is true," said Damase. "He would never dare to strike you; but we aren't all you, Gabriel."

GABRIEL DUMONT'S HOMESTEAD,
BURNED DOWN BY THE TROOPS,
MAY 8, 1885

The two buildings on the left constituted Dumont's dwelling house—the two on the right, his store. The building to the extreme right was his warehouse. Two stables in the rear of the dwelling and store were also burned. One hundred and fifty yards away is the Saskatchewan, with Dumont's famous ferry.

JOHN KERR, *friend*

In his own home Gabriel was never quarrelsome, and so far as I ever knew or heard, his wife and adopted daughter—he had no children of his own—never heard an unkind word from him. He adored them.

Madeleine and I put up a signpost where the Carlton Trail forked, forty miles east of Gabriel's Crossing. It told everyone that my ferry was the best one on the river and that using it shaved twenty-five miles off the route to Battleford. Madeleine wrote it in English, French, and Cree, and we printed up an advertisement.

MAXIMUM RATES OF FERRY TOLLS CHARGEABLE FOR
CARRYING UNDER THIS LICENSE SHALL BE:

		Cents
1)	For every single vehicle, loaded or unloaded, including one horse, or other animal, and driver	25
2)	For every double vehicle, loaded or unloaded, including two horses, or two other animals, and driver	50
3)	For every horse and its rider	20
4)	For every horse, mule, ox, or cow (not included with vehicle or rider)	10
5)	For every sheep, hog, calf, or colt	5
6)	For every passenger in vehicle (except team driver, as above)	5
7)	For every passenger on foot	10
8)	For all articles or goods, not in a vehicle, over one hundred pounds, per one hundred pounds	2

Gabriel Dumont will double these rates if he sees fit to ferry anyone over between dusk and dawn. On Sundays between nine in the morning and two in the afternoon free crossing will be provided for all churchgoers.

FATHER ALEXIS ANDRÉ, *priest*

In 1871 the Métis community settled near Duck Lake, which I named St. Laurent, grew so much that Bishop Grandin stationed me here permanently. Many of the people had moved directly to St. Laurent from La Petite Ville. By 1872 my flock seemed bountiful and might have formed a grand and successful Mission if my parishioners had stayed in one place. Unfortunately, most of these Métis had only moved from the Red River in order to hunt the buffaloes more easily. I got worried that they might move again, farther out on the prairies where the buffaloes take shelter more frequently these days. The buffaloes will in time completely disappear, of course, but in the meantime I know that I must convince my Métis to form temporary organizations of their own to regulate justice and resolve the disputes that arise among them. With time such organizations will aid them to make the shift to agriculture.

I have worked hard to bring this about. On the last day of 1871, the communities of the South Branch held a meeting. Lawrence Clarke, the agent for the Hudson's Bay Company at Fort Carlton, was invited to be president. I acted as secretary for the meeting and recorded his words:

I can assure this meeting that whatever steps you take to form a permanent Colony, you will have the best wishes and sympathies of the Chief Officer of the Hudson's Bay Company in the Country, Mister Donald A. Smith. And you know the excellent work he did for the Manitoba Métis in 1869. You have met to decide whether you will continue to lead savage lives. Will you continue, like the Indians, to wander from year to year following the Buffalo? Are you content to eke out a precarious living from the muzzle of your guns? Content to isolate yourselves from all the benefits derived from the duties and consolations of your religion? Will you prevent your children from receiving the education without which they can never hope to rise in the world, but must remain forever the slaves of their more intelligent fellow citizens?

I tell you that should such be your decision, then you proclaim your own national and political demise. This country is even now changing and in a few years will be peopled by hordes of energetic, industrious men from other countries. You know, as well if not better than myself, that the Buffalo are fast decreasing and will be completely destroyed before another generation has passed away. What then have your children to look forward to? I will tell you: abject poverty, deep misery, and ultimate extermination. Follow your present course of life for a few more years, and it does not require much foresight to predict your destinies. You will be scattered far and wide over the land, gleaning a miserable existence from the depleted waters of its lakes and rivers, or begging from your more industrious neighbours. Your future is in your own hands, and as you decide today, so will you in the future be—either a happy or a miserable people.

I do not ask you, immediately, to change your way of life radically. That would be folly. I only ask you now, before the best sections of this country are taken up by strangers, to establish your land claims and fix yourselves on them permanently. Abandon your wanderings and settle down to a stable livelihood. Rely on the hunt, on your farms, *and* on freighting. Then, should one or two fail, you will have a third to fall back upon. I ask you, in the names of your children whose future welfare you must all have at heart, to carry out the purposes for which you have assembled here. Found your Colony, build churches and schools, have your children trained and educated to labour intelligently, that they may carry your names down to posterity without disgrace or reproach.

Before asking you to record your votes for or against tonight's resolutions, I call your attention to the conditions they impose on you. This is a democracy. Your committees are your representatives and you *must* bind yourselves without further demure to accept their decisions as conclusive. If you vote for these Resolutions now, you will have no right to withdraw when the time comes to act in founding your Colony. Remember, it is only by working together in accord and unity that you can hope to prosper, and I reiterate that you will be guilty of a *crime* against your brothers should you withdraw from the compact you now publicly enter into. If there are any amongst you who are not willing to bind themselves, they should abstain from voting.

When Mr. Clarke had finished speaking I said that Bishop Grandin was on our side and I endorsed the soundness of Mr. Clarke's views. So long as they were dispersed, the Métis could never become a nation. I asked if they had gathered with the full determination to found a Métis Colony. Would they abide by and carry out all the Resolutions that had been proposed at this meeting, and would they express their satisfaction with them by show of hands? When every hand in the room went high with loud cheering, Mr. Clarke said, "We are now, gentlemen, no longer simple traders or hunters, but Colonists."

I attended the meeting that Father André called at St. Laurent and heard what Mr. Lawrence Clarke said. He promised that he would represent our interests. I believed the priest when he said that Bishop Grandin was on our side. So answer, if you can, why the Government refused us land enough for a reserve?

By 1873, when Lieutenant-Governor Alexander Morris took Mennonites to White Horse Plain in search of farmland, I knew we were in trouble. We had written letters and petitions, and sent our representatives to the Government, and now we grew alarmed. Métis had been settled at White Horse Plain for fifty years, but the Government showed that land to new immigrants. And the Mennonites got their reserves.

DONALD A. SMITH ESQUIRE
Chief Commissioner
Hudson's Bay Company
Fort Garry
January 1872

Dear Sir:

I have to repeat for your information that, by a pressing invitation on the 31st of December, I presided at a meeting of the French halfbreed population wintering in the South Saskatchewan River, at which it was resolved by all present that, in the interests of themselves and their families, they should abandon their wandering habits and fix themselves at or near Carlton as a permanent Colony. There are, scattered in small hamlets through the plains country of the lower

Saskatchewan, about two hundred and fifty heads of families who have decided to unite and form themselves into one Grand Settlement. Ten of the most respected of their people have been chosen as a Committee to examine in early spring and fix upon the site for the new plantation, which will immediately thereafter be built upon by them.

This Colony, once started, will rapidly become strong and influential. The founders are not poor men. They are rich in horses and all have more or less money at their disposal. The decision they have arrived at will have a most important bearing upon our trade here, and must benefit us in every branch of our business.

As Carriers for the Northern districts, they will ensure us a reliable source from which to draw all the Freighters we may require. And as the Settlement increases in population, so will competition arise amongst them for fuller employment in this, their favourite occupation. That will enable us to reduce the rates of freight to a minimum standard, directly saving a large sum of money annually.

Indirectly, we shall profit by this location insomuch that, getting our transport carried so cheaply, we will be able to dispense with a transport establishment of our own, and all the enormous expenses and ruinous losses yearly incurred thereby. We will save on our outlay for oxen, carts, harnesses, and agents, and be enabled to reduce our staff of employees to a third of our present force, thus indirectly diminishing our expenditure, at the lowest calculation, by two thousand pounds sterling per annum.

I am, dear Sir,
Your Obedient Servant,
L. CLARKE

Government House

Fort Garry

January 1872

My dear Sir:

Referring to Bishop Grandin, he must have entirely misunderstood the conversation he had with me if he imagined that I authorized him to lay off any Half Breed reserve. The only Half Breed Claim is that which is created by the Act of Manitoba, and that is confined to Manitoba.

What I said was, I had no doubt that the Government would recognize the claims of actual settlers to an amount of land reasonably sufficient to make a farm for each head of a family—and, in reply to the question about how settlers could prevent interference from strangers coming in, I told him there would be no difficulty in the occupants marking off their land and holding it by lines. How he could have supposed that the liberty of settlers to retain their holdings and a reasonable surrounding area could be construed to mean the reservation of half a province is something incomprehensible to me. There has been trouble enough with Half Breed Reserves in Manitoba to warn us against a revival of the same troubles outside.

A claim of such a tract as you speak of, say 140 miles by 20 miles, equal to an area of 1,800,000 acres, requires only to be stated to show its absurdity. No Government and no Government Officer could entertain such a proposition.

These people can found no claim upon their being Half Breeds. It is only as Settlers that any indulgence can be shown them. And how can one settler say to another, as you say has been done out there: "My right is better than yours." No man located there can be disturbed, and any settler there has the same right, whether White, Half Breed, or Indian. Your own judgement will tell you this.

Anybody who goes to Saskatchewan to settle has just as much right to enter on unoccupied land as those had who went before them, and I shall not be sorry to see a goodly amount of immigration for settlement there next spring.

As to the question of Legislation, any community may make rules for its own Government, and so long as the people choose to abide by them, no harm is done. They have no power, however, to enforce these rules if anyone resists them. As to any regulations it may be considered desirable to be able to enforce, the best plan will be to forward a copy of them to me, accompanied by an affidavit certifying that they were adopted at a meeting where the wishes of the inhabitants were fairly ascertained, and I shall take the necessary steps to give them force of law.

I can not assume to judge whether mischiefs might be made of this matter. Possibly it might be the best course, so soon as I receive an official statement of what has been done, to write myself to the Bishop to tell him he has entirely misconceived the tenor of my conversation with him.

Believe me, my dear Sir,
Yours very truly,
A.G. ARCHIBALD
Lieutenant Governor

St. Laurent: Little huts promiscuously huddled together; horses, dogs, women, children, all intermixed in confusion; half-breed hunters, ribboned and tasseled, lazy, idle, and, if there is any alcohol in the camp, sure to be drunk; remnants and wrecks of buffalo scattered everywhere, stretched robes drying, sheets of meat hanging on stages, wolf-skins spread over frames; women carrying water and wood, and as the light dies the glow of firelight through parchment windows and the scraping sound of fiddles; then comes the quick thud of heels as Louis and Baptiste or Gabriel splinter the half-hewn floors.

So my Métis settled themselves at St. Laurent and got on with their lives. In mid winter of 1873 I was camped near St. Laurent when a passing Cree heard the throb of the drum in my tent. The young man listened and was lost. He sat down opposite me for a game. At first he won, but Fortune soon turned against him and before evening he gambled away everything he had.

A few days later John Kerr tracked me down. He said, "Gabriel, I have discovered a family of Crees starving a few miles south of St. Laurent." I told Kerr to return the next morning and we would do something about them. He left to smoke and visit with Louis Marion. Then across they went to Philip Gariépuy's tent. Philip was a kindly man, and he also agreed that something must be done. By morning the whole camp knew the situation—which shows how quickly news spreads in a Métis camp.

At dawn we discussed the problem and visited Father André. Kerr did not speak French well, and the priest questioned him till he lost patience and exclaimed in English to Louis Marion, "Oh hell, let's go!" Basil Poitras did not speak English any better than Kerr spoke French, and he thought that Kerr had told the priest to go to hell. Poitras immediately attacked him, but Kerr was a very good wrestler, so Poitras was soon on his back. I pulled them apart.

We returned to Gabriel's Crossing, where Madeleine got some meat from our storehouse—a leg of buffalo and half a sack of pemmican. She grumbled and told me not to be always giving things away; but many was the winter we ourselves had been hungry and her grumbling did not mean anything, especially when she heard there were children starving. I loaded the food on a sled and, since Kerr said that the Cree hunter was ill, I went back to the priest for some medicine.

Inside the tipi I found the gambler who had lost everything to me a few days earlier. His wife and two small children looked relieved when we brought in the grub. Father André, who had accompanied us, mixed medicine for the sick man. When that hunter was well enough to travel, he brought a sleeping robe and offered it to me. I had plenty of fine buffalo robes and would not accept it, but that says something about our life on the prairie. Indian, White man, or Métis, we tried to make certain that no one starved if someone else had food. And everyone always tried to give something for what they got. Things changed forever when the English built their towns—townsmen against *les sauvages*; Whites against Indians and Métis; them against us.

Madeleine and I were married in the early summer of 1858, the year my mother died. Father Joseph Goiffon performed the ceremony at the start of the spring hunt, at St. Joe, in Dakota Territory. Madeleine wore a white blouse and a forest-green skirt, with a scarlet vest and a sky-blue ribbon in her black hair. The children covered her in wildflowers.

All my jealous friends told me how fortunate I was. They asked how an ugly animal like me had captured such a lovely wife. "I can hunt," I told them. What a time our honeymoon was. Lucky I wasn't killed running the buffalo that year—Madeleine was the only thing on my mind. I couldn't keep my hands off her.

Life was good in those days. In those days everyone danced, and there were fiddlers in every Métis camp. On our dance floors— green buffalo hides pegged to the prairie—we danced the Métis dances: the Red River Jig, the Reel of Four, the Reel of Eight, the Double Jig, Strip the Willow, Rabbit Chase, Tucker Circle, Drops of Brandy. There were fancy dances, too, but the main thing was to lift your feet. The Red River Jig was the quickest.

Toward the end of each party there was always a Rabbit-Chase where the men and women stood in two rows. One couple danced between the rows and parted at the end—the woman behind the women's row, and the man behind the men's. When they got half-way back, the man chased his partner until he caught her. Then it started all over again, and this time the woman did the chasing. Every dancer got a turn.

For the Handkerchief Dance, a man took a handkerchief in his hand and looped it around a woman's neck, then they danced together and he kissed her. Then she danced around the floor behind her partner, chose another partner, looped the hand-kerchief around his neck and kissed him. So it went until every man and woman had been kissed. The Handkerchief Dance wound up each party.

Three years after our defeat at Batoche I spoke to a crowd in Montréal. I was speaking on behalf of Honoré Mercier, and the people of Quebec were outraged by the injustices the Métis had suffered. A fire broke out while I was speaking, and we rushed from the lecture hall out into the street. Screams drifted from a nearby house. I climbed through the flames to the upper apartments and helped some small children descend to safety.

When I was back on the street someone asked: "Why did you endanger yourself like that? You did not know those people. You did not know how dangerous that fire was."

"How could I think of myself," I answered, "hearing little children crying out for help? Is suffering so unreal to you? Starving ragged beggars, screaming children—don't you feel compassion for them? Those crying children were my Métis. Intelligent people must not look away from suffering. Step outside yourself and you will find us on any street."

It is always the same—French or English. It is safer to speak about virtue than to display it.

Peter Ballentine was one of us. He attended all our rendezvous and meetings and knew the St. Laurent laws. So also did Baptiste Primeau, Alexander Cadien, and Theodore Covenant. But Lawrence Clarke got to them. Clarke could not accept that we were free people, leaving him with no power over us. He outfitted Ballentine and the others and sent them on ahead of our St. Laurent caravan. Madeleine helped me write the letter calling them back to the Great Camp. It was in English, so Clarke would understand when he read it.

17 June 1875

My friends,

We are not satisfied that you travel before us, nor that you are hunting in our Country.

Therefore, all the Métis people of Carlton pray that you come at once to our camp. If you do not agree, our horsemen will come and forcibly bring you to our camp; and if you cause them any trouble you will pay them for it. That concerns especially the Métis of your camp.

We write to you as friends, to advise you. If you do not believe us, certainly you will pay the horsemen who come to get you.

> *Farewell,*
> *Your servants,*
> GABRIEL DUMONT
> *and all the Métis people from*
> *Carlton camped on the plains*

PETER BALLENTINE, *Métis renegade*

On the 19th of June 1875, forty-one armed men visited our camp, all of them on horseback and armed to the teeth with fourteen- and sixteen-stroke repeating rifles, to take us all to their Camp; and if we refused to go they said that they would force us to go. After some small talk, one of their leaders rose and said, "What is the use of talking? We came here to take them. Let us do what we said we would do." Gabriel Dumont then said, "Go! Harness their horses and load their carts and take them to the Great Camp." All of them got up and went to our tents and hustled our things into the carts. We told them that they had better think seriously about what they were doing; that their best course would be to leave us alone. Then the call went up: "Start the carts!" And, of course, they started. Gabriel Dumont again turned to us and said, "Get in the carts." But our men said they would not go; that they would not recognize the laws of the hunt, but would see what the Government had to say; and that they hoped that they would obtain justice that way. Gabriel Dumont then halted the carts and said, "Fine them." So they helped themselves, and took from our loads whatever they wanted.

POLICE INSPECTOR LEIF CROZIER,
to Police Commissioner French

On the 20th of August, I received a letter from the principal men of St. Laurent asking me to attend a meeting so that they might explain the rules and regulations they had established for their guidance. I attended the meeting in company with Mr. Clarke, Justice of the Peace, before whom the information was laid in the Dumont matter.

These men gave me a copy of their laws and wished me particularly to understand that they had no intention of doing anything that was illegal or wrong. In the absence of a protective Force in the Country, they explained that they thought they were justified in making these laws.

Dumont, the president against whom the information was laid before Mr. Clarke, was present at the meeting. He apologized for having fined men detached from his own party. Because he at once offered to return the money and make any other reparation necessary to the complainants, Mr. Clarke and I considered, subject to your approval, that it was better not to arrest him.

From what I saw of these people, I am sure that they are loyal and law-abiding and are anxious that the Government send Magistrates before whom they can legally settle their differences. The people of the settlement are also anxious that the Government should make hunting laws as soon as possible.

I did not find it humiliating to apologize to Crozier. I had been elected to enforce the St. Laurent laws, so we punished Ballentine and Primeau. They knew the law: they were Métis and the St. Laurent hunt was the largest party on the prairie; they were obliged to hunt with us or not at all. I had no intention of letting Clarke settle the case, because by then I suspected that he himself had outfitted them. And Crozier was wise to let the matter drop after I apologized. Remember this: first Selby Smyth and his men came to Gabriel's Crossing to speak with me, then Crozier came in front of *my* Council. They did not arrest me. I *never* let them decide what was just, and they knew better than to send policemen to try and bring me in. I was elected to protect the Colony, and that is what I was doing. The Council paid the fines that the police imposed on me.

EDWARD BLAKE, *Minister of Justice for the Government of Canada*
With reference to the application of such of the St. Laurent laws as apply to men other than those engaged in the great hunt, both custom and reason would appear to indicate the necessity of *some* regulation, inasmuch as the presence in the

neighbourhood of a few independent hunters would render utterly useless the regulations of the Great Camp, and prevent the capture of the buffalo.

The only acts which Commissioner French can find done with reference to others than the members of the organization had regard to hunting regulations. One incident occurred last year; the other in the spring of this year. The principal individual in the party apprehended this year, a man named Primeau, had belonged to the St. Laurent Colony, and it was he who laid information against Dumont.

Neither incident afforded any adequate ground for the statements made by Mister Clarke and confirmed by Mister Graham—unless their objection to the latest incident lies in the fact that Clarke himself had outfitted the apprehended party and sent it on ahead of the St. Laurent camp in order, apparently, to steal a march on the Great Camp.

There does not appear to have been the slightest foundation for the alarm expressed by those Gentlemen, or the least justification for the pressing communication which resulted in the hurried expedition that Inspector Crozier led to Carlton. I submit to Council that the Lieutenant Governor of the North West Territories should be requested to call on Mister Clarke for any explanation he may have to offer of his conduct, and that, unless satisfactory explanations are made, the Government should in some way mark its disapprobation of the conduct of Mister Clarke and Mister Graham.

FRANCIS DICKENS, *policeman*

How the man spotted me I cannot guess, but before I knew it he was standing over me. I scrambled up, brushing off my trousers. He was a noble-looking savage, barrel-chested and wearing a fringed hide jacket decorated with handsome needlework floral designs in the Métis style. Long, dark hair curled down his neck. His face was nut-brown and unwrinkled, and his blazing eyes would have daunted a panther. He seemed both resolute and faintly cavalier, clearly a Métis, but one such as I had never met before.

"Good evening, sir," I said.

He nodded and murmured, "*Ne bouge pas.*" He then pointed his rifle straight at my head. In horror I watched him squeeze the trigger. I closed my eyes and braced myself, but the bullet winged past my ear and I opened my eyes to find him fifty yards away stooping to pick up a prairie chicken. Silently he held it out, displaying with a flourish the fact that with his hunting rifle he had shot the head cleanly off it.

Before I could decide whether to admire the man's marksmanship or complain that he had deafened me, we were joined by an elderly villager whose day's fishing had, on the evidence, proved barren.

"*B'jour, José,*" rumbled the Métis. "*Tiens.*" He handed the bird to the old man.

"*Merci, Gabriel, merci!*" The old man ambled off, cradling his prize. I, however, felt a fresh tremor of anxiety. This could only be Gabriel Dumont. Even Sam Steele had spoken that name with reverence. The nearest crossing-point upriver was named after this Nimrod.

Dumont was of particular interest to the Justice Ministry at this time, which had issued a warrant for his arrest (prudently ignored by us law officers) for having assaulted a member of a band of buffalo hunters. The hunter had violated "the law of the plains." One hunter trying to steal a march on the others could stampede several thousand buffalo. For having enforced this ancient law, Dumont had received an admonitory lecture from Sir E. Selby Smyth.

On thinking of Smyth I felt such an immediate bond with Dumont that I could not restrain myself from blurting out, "Major-General Sir E. Selby Smyth!"—and holding my nose in the universal gesture of distaste. Dumont roared with laughter. "*Bien sûr!*" he said, and held *his* nose. There we stood, in an enchanted moment of communion, each holding his nose in an evening whose aroma was beyond reproach.

Delighted as I am to recall my brief encounter with that intelligent, jovial man, I admit to being disquieted by his aura of authority and command. Better for us policemen were this river's boatman an ancient whose only purpose was to ferry souls to whatever Hades lies on the west bank of the Saskatchewan.

Madeleine and I were very happy. She taught school in Batoche and rode out every morning to her babies. Back she came each night with all their little sayings to share with me. Our family had grown bigger than we had ever dared hope.

This summer I planted ten acres in potatoes and barley. The ferry gave me more work than I wanted. We lived pretty good without the hunting. In 1880 or 1881, I led the last Saskatchewan hunts, but *les animaux* were gone and our ancient ways went with them.

In 1876, hundreds of tipis surrounded Fort Carlton for the treaty gathering. Dust hung in the yellow air. On the second day, a police band marched in—a group of warriors met it and wanted to trade for the drum.

Peter Erasmus interpreted for the police. Madeleine came along to interpret for me. Of all the chiefs, only Big Bear was determined enough to speak out, but he was not at Carlton. He was out conferring with the Crees and Assiniboines on the prairie so he could carry their thoughts as well as his own. He was late for Fort Pitt, too, because the Government didn't think it was important to wait for him. But we heard about the speech he gave.

"My friends," he said, "I heard the Governor was here and I came to see him. I wanted to ask him to save us from what I most dread: that someone will lead us by a rope about the neck."

By a rope, Big Bear meant losing his liberty—the way a wild horse is led by a rope about its neck; the treaty was the rope the Government was putting on the Indians. At the end Big Bear repeated: "I tell you that I do not want a rope on me. *Nemoia, ay-saka-pay-kinit*—do not lead me where I do not want to go."

My brothers Jean and Isidore signed the Fort Carlton treaty as witnesses, but I refused. It was unjust and would bring only trouble on the Indians. By then I knew we needed a leader who understood the English, who could speak to the lawyers and politicians in ways they understood. Riel had already forced one good treaty from the Canadians in 1869.

The last hunt I led was a bad one for us. The robe hunters and the U.S. Cavalry burned the prairie south of the line, and the buffalo herds never returned to the Saskatchewan. Then in the fall the Canadians tried to charge us for the wood we cut, so I searched out Louis Schmidt and told him it could not go on. "There is nothing we can make them do about it," he said. "The law is passed."

I would not accept this answer. Some others and I, we called a meeting at Batoche. I reminded the Métis about our St. Laurent Colony. I told them, "You left Manitoba because the Government would not leave you alone, and you came to this new, wild country. Where else can you go? You came as far as you could. Now they want us to pay for wood to burn. We must take a stand. If we permit the Government to do this, it will never stop."

The meeting decided to draw up another petition, and Father Vegreville helped us do it. At that time Michel Dumas worked for the Government. We called him the Rat. He was the agent who seized our wood. When he tried to sign our petition, I said, "We don't need your signature. You look like a Métis, but you smell like an enemy."

"But Mr. Dumont," he said, "I want to show my sympathy."

I held the petition away from him. Then my Uncle Isidore took the petition. "Go away," he said to Dumas. "Can't you see that Gabriel does not want you here?"

Lawrence Clarke was still our representative on the district assembly. I took the petition to him at Fort Carlton and said, "This is too much. You are our elected representative. Surely even you can see it is not right for us to have to pay for wood in this wild country. If you don't do something now, more rules will follow."

Clarke said that all the representatives had voted, and no one had disapproved then.

I said, "If it is law, then you must work to abolish it. You must do this for us. Otherwise, what do we need a representative for?"

"No," said Clarke. "There is nothing I can do. It is not worth the effort to try."

I gave him the petition and said, "Here! Try! Take our petition to Winnipeg. And hurry up, we do not have much time."

When Clarke saw the petition and all our signatures he said, "You didn't tell me about this. With this petition, I can help you. I will telegraph Winnipeg and if I don't get an answer, then I will let the Government pay my way there."

In five days, we had an order permitting us to cut all the wood we needed. Michel Dumas received the news, and a few days later he met my brother Jean, whose wood he had seized. Jean was cutting more wood, and Dumas said that he could have his other wood back. My brother said, "The moment we went to work against you, Rat, I knew that I would get my wood back. Today is a good day for me."

We had won, but we heard some bad news too. To humiliate him and us, the Government had locked poor Louis Riel in a lunatic asylum.

JAMES TROW, *MP and Chairman of the Immigration and Colonization Committee of the House of Commons*:

Early September 1877 (in a thick fog)—We arrived at Dumont's Ferry and, having no horn, whistled for Gabriel. We could not see twenty feet ahead. The rude ferryman soon appeared and made preparations for crossing. His famous ferry was a flat-bottomed scow, roughly put together. Our animals were unhitched, the carriage and cart put in the centre of the boat, with the mules on one side and the horses on the other. Gabriel gave his gruff instructions by signs and in some very doubtful French. The mules were obstinate and troublesome. He was probably more accustomed to oxen than to mules and undertook to twist the tail of one of the mules. Instantly he received a sound kick below the ribs, in that portion of the body called by pugilists "the bread basket." When Dumont was quite recovered from the blow, each of our party undertook to row the unyielding oars, first keeping along the shore and working upstream. Fortunately, the wind was favourable, which counteracted the force of the rapid current. The Saskatchewan has a swift current and is over two hundred yards in width at low water, with an average depth of eight to fifteen feet. The fee we paid Gabriel was $1.50 for ourselves, our horses, and our carriages—not too much to pay. All in all, an amusing encounter with one leader of the noble Métis of the Saskatchewan.

For some years we had been getting regular visits from Government agents. In August 1881, Lord Lorne, who was Governor General of all Canada, arrived in the Saskatchewan. He stopped at my house, and I took it as an honour that he visited me. I ferried his whole company across the river myself: eighty horses and nineteen wagons. There was a heavy wind this day. All the buffalo hunters and their women had collected at Batoche to greet him, but he was three days late and they had all gone off to hunt by the time he arrived. After I moved him across the river I joined the few other Métis leaders who still remained and accompanied him as far as Duck Lake, where Lawrence Clarke waited to address him on our behalf. The next day Madeleine and I watched the great Lord speak with the Indians. Then he got on the *Northcote* and steamed down river and we heard nothing more from him.

About this same time, settlers began stealing land from the Edmonton Métis. About thirty Métis families were forced off their farms. When they reported the problem to the police, they were told that nothing could be done. They petitioned, accusing the Government of ignoring their rights and giving their land to invaders, but they knew that they would only get justice if they took it for themselves. So they rode out on horse-back and threatened to pull down the new houses. The new settlers were upset. The Métis had no intention of backing down and came very close to spilling blood. When we learned of their fate, we worried that the Government would treat us the same way. We did not want to fight for our rights, as we had in 1869, but we had grown resolved to hold firm.

To: RIGHT HONOURABLE SIR JOHN A. MACDONALD
Prime Minister of Canada
and Minister of the Interior
From: ST. ANTOINE DE PADOUE,
South Saskatchewan River
September 4, 1882

Sir: Compelled, most of us, to abandon the prairie, which can no longer furnish us the means of subsistence, we came in large numbers and settled on the south branch of the Saskatchewan. The surveyed lands being already occupied, we were compelled to occupy lands not yet surveyed, being ignorant, for the most part, also, of the regulations respecting Dominion lands. Great then was our astonishment and perplexity when we were notified that, when the lands are surveyed, we shall be obliged to pay \$2 an acre to the Government if our lands are included in odd-numbered sections. We desire, moreover, to keep close together, in order more easily to secure a school and a church.

We are poor people and can not pay for our land without utter ruin, and losing the fruits of our labour or seeing our lands pass into the hands of strangers, who will go to the land office at Prince Albert and pay the amount fixed by the Government. In our anxiety, we appeal to your sense of justice as Minister of the Interior and head of the Government, and beg you to reassure us speedily, by directing that we shall not be disturbed on our lands, and that the Government will grant the privilege of considering us as occupants of even-numbered sections, since we have occupied these lands in good faith.

Having so long held this country as its masters and so often defended it against the Indians at the price of our blood, we request that the Government allow us to occupy our lands in peace, and that exception be made to its regulations, by giving the half-breeds of the North West free grants of lands. We also pray that you will direct that the lots be surveyed along the river ten chains in width by two miles in depth, this mode of division being the long-established usage of the country.

We trust, Sir, that you will grant a favourable hearing to this our petition, and that you will make known your decision as soon as possible. We await it with great anxiety and pray God to protect you and keep you for the direction of this great Country which you so wisely govern.

Your humble petitioners,
GABRIEL DUMONT,
JEAN CARON,
EMMANUEL CHAMPAGNE,
LOUISON BATOCHE,
and forty-two others

ARCHBISHOP ALEXANDRE TACHÉ,
to Prime Minister Sir John A. Macdonald

The formidable Indian question has not yet risen in our midst, owing largely to the influence of the Halfbreeds. The disappearance of the buffalo and especially the movement of the settlers into the Indian country, are generating difficulties that may be avoided, I hope, but which will otherwise involve such terrible and expensive results that it is the duty of all the friends of the Government and of the country to do all in their power to prevent them.

The result will depend in a great measure on the way the Halfbreeds are treated. When friendly, they contribute mightily to the maintenance of peace; dissatisfied, they would not only add to the difficulty, but render the settlement of the country next to impossible.

The Halfbreeds are a highly sensitive race; they keenly resent injury or insult, and daily complain on that point. In fact, they are daily humiliated with regard to their origin by the way they are spoken of, not only in the newspapers but also in official and semi-official documents. The Halfbreed question must be decided upon without further delay. There is no doubt the difficulties will only increase with time.

3

We held several meetings during 1882 and 1883 to let everyone speak who wanted to. Our decisions were unanimous—we would not act until we had convinced everyone. We knew that the Government had plans for us Métis. However hard we worked to satisfy their regulations, they intended to take our land from us. The way Abraham Montour was treated proves this.

Montour had cultivated a farm near Batoche since 1873, but in the summer of 1883 a man named Johnson rode out from Prince Albert and told him to leave. Johnson said that the Government had sold him the farm. Montour drove Johnson away and told the rest of us what had happened. We were outraged.

After this news, we had a meeting at the house of my father. We had been working on a Bill of Rights, but now my father demanded to know how we could take some real action. Everyone agreed: Louis Riel was the only man who could seize the attention of the Government. We voted to ask him back. We wanted a treaty like the one he had negotiated for Manitoba. To the Canadians Riel was like a drowned man: he was never in sight, but every time they tried to fire their guns over us Métis he rolled to the surface and made a stink. We knew we could count on him.

Jimmie Ibister and I were delegated to go to Montana, which is where Riel went after he was released from the lunatic asylum. The whole Métis community promised to care for our families while we were gone. Moïse Ouellette and Michel Dumas offered to join us because they wanted to meet Riel, and we agreed that they would add their voices to ours in case he needed more persuading. Lafontaine and Gariépuy were on their way to Lewiston to look for Lafontaine's mother, so they accompanied us part of the way. I had a simple Métis cart, and Moïse and Jimmie each had double-hitch wagons.

Lawrence Clarke said that if I went to find Riel he would see that the police put me in jail. I laughed in his face. It was my first trip to Montana, but I somehow knew exactly how long it would take to reach Riel. Before I left I told the council, "The fifteenth day after we leave here, we will be near him." We slipped off quietly on the 19th of May, and on the morning of June 4th we reached Saint Peter's Mission.

LOUIS GOULET, *plainsman*

On the 24th of March 1884, Gabriel Dumont and José Vandal invited me to attend a meeting at the house of Abraham Montour, in Batoche. I hitched up my carriage and took Vandal with me; Dumont rode on alone.

Gabriel Dumont was chairman at that meeting of thirty men, with Michel Dumas as secretary. Dumont began by explaining why the meeting had been called. He warned us that the assembly was secret, that we must all take an oath of secrecy, and that everyone must speak his whole mind.

After we had been sworn in, Dumont explained our political situation. Although he had no formal education, he had a first-class mind and spoke with extraordinary ease. His strong, vibrant voice could grip the attention of any audience. Whenever he talked in Cree, which he did that night, he held his listeners in the palm of his hand.

He explained why the Métis of the North West deserved the same treatment as the Métis of Manitoba. He reminded us that we had set out our grievances for the Governor General of the Dominion when he had come west. We had told him that we never received any land grants, as the Manitoba Métis had by virtue of their Indian ancestry. Even those who had been settled on farms for fifteen or twenty years and more had never received their titles. Moreover, government agents made them pay for hay and wood they cut on lands which should belong to them twice over, once as natural children of the country by right of their Indian birth, and again by right of settlement and first occupancy.

He spoke for a long time about the miseries and injustices the Métis had endured since the day they had let the English set themselves up as lords of the land. He recalled the Governor General's promise to settle our claims justly. "That was many years ago," Dumont said, "and we have nothing to show for it; in spite of all our petitions to Ottawa; in spite of all the approaches we made and caused to be made to the Government. And let me tell you, my friends, the Canadians will never give us anything! They stole our land with promises, and now they are laughing at us. They will not grant us the slightest thing in return for soil where generations of our ancestors sleep, unless we force justice from them."

Dumont recalled his efforts since 1870 in trying to organize the Indians and encourage them to present a united front in the face of the White invasion. He admitted he was not well enough educated to inspire confidence and said, "Before I sit down, I want to tell you that there is one man who *can* do what I want to do, and that is Louis Riel. Let us bring him back from Montana."

We all agreed with everything Dumont said. I myself had thought about those same issues for a long time, but, like Dumont, I did not have the qualities it takes to lead a movement. Charles Nolin spoke for all of us when he thanked

Dumont for setting out the truth so well. "The problem with us Métis right now," Nolin said, "is that we are a cart with only one wheel. If we want to get moving, we will have to fetch the other one we need from Montana."

Nolin's speech was not on the same level as Dumont's, but it was full of good sense. We decided unanimously that Dumont was the best man to send after Riel. At that point, somebody reminded us that a trip to Montana would be long and costly and dangerous, and if Dumont went he would need at least one companion who knew the country they would be travelling through. "We have the man he will need here with us now," said the speaker. "Louis Goulet just got back from the Missouri. He knows that country like the back of his hand—knows Riel and exactly where he is."

I told the meeting that I was honoured and thanked them, but I could not go because I had just signed a contract to carry the mail for the surveyors in the Battle River area. My excuse was a good one. Nolin suggested that we first raise the money that two or three men would need for the trip. We decided to call another meeting to discuss the question of money and consider who should go with Dumont.

On my way back home, I was feeling good. The reason I had given for not going with Dumont was a good one, but there was another I did not want to mention. I had never liked Riel. My father had opposed him in 1870, and I myself had wrangled with him more than once over trading liquor. He was dead against it. Because of that past history, I was afraid that my presence in the delegation might do more harm than good to the Métis cause. In justice to Riel's memory, I must say that after I got to know him better I realized there was no such worry. Riel was not the kind of man to hold a grudge or drag up old disputes. But I did not know as much that evening.

Resolutions Agreed upon at the Public Assembly at the Home of
Isidore Dumont, on the 21st April 1884.

We, the French and English natives, being convinced that
the Government of Canada has taken possession of the North-
West Territories without the consent of the natives, both
French and English, claim as our rights:

1) that we receive at least the same rights and privileges as
   claimed by the natives of Manitoba, seeing that the
   North-West is much wealthier in resources;

2) that we be represented in the North-West council, based
   on the native population living here;

3) that the French and English natives of the North-West
   (those that have not participated in the Manitoba lands
   grant) are entitled to free Patent for the lands they
   possess and occupy at the present date—without preju-
   dice toward more land grants to which they are entitled
   for the extinction of their Indian title to the lands of the
   North-West;

4) that the natives, French and English, reject payment of
   all dues and charges on the timber and forests until all
   their rights mentioned herein be recognized and granted
   by the Dominion Government;

5) that the management of the Indians' affairs such as Indian
   Agents, Instructorships, or other offices for the benefit of
   the Indians in the North-West Territories be entrusted to
   natives, as they are more familiar with the habits, character, and wants of those Indians, and to prevent any
   regrettable occurrences as have happened in the past;

6) that the French and English natives of the North-West,
   having never recognized any right to the lands of this
   North-West assumed by the Hudson's Bay Company or

by the Dominion Government, claim an exclusive right to those lands along with the Indians;

7) that knowing that Louis Riel made a bargain with the Government of Canada in 1870, which said bargain is contained mostly in what is known as "the Manitoba Act," and not knowing the contents of said "Manitoba Act," we have thought it advisable that a delegation be sent to Louis Riel to invite his assistance to bring all the matters referred to in the above resolutions into proper shape and form before the Government of Canada, so that our just demands be granted.

Dim and smoky morning buckles until the prairie joins the sky. So strange. So strange. A world turning upside down. On floating horses we ride across the clouds watching the shifting world beneath us, like phantoms riding a milky way.

It was a difficult journey. There were mountains and ravines to cross, and prairies and rivers, but most dangerous of all were the Indians. The Blackfoot permitted us to pass, but the Gros Ventre in Montana had never smoked my tobacco. One small band of warriors stopped us on the south bank of the Milk River and demanded that we surrender our horses. Petite Blanche Tête was their chief.

"Young warriors," I said, "you must think about what you do. We have friends awaiting us, and others know where we are. If you try to take my horses you must kill me, and I won't die easily. Some of you will die too. I am a chief of my people. I once defeated your great chief Bull's Hide in personal combat, and now he is my friend. We smoked the pipe together. He will become your enemy if you interfere with me. And some of the men here with me will surely survive this fight and tell the U.S. Cavalry what you have done. Then the soldiers will hunt you like animals. Let us pass. Smoke with us, and let us pass. Our business is not with you."

Because Mass had just begun, it must have been exactly 8 o'clock in the morning when we entered the courtyard of Saint Peter's Mission. I spoke to an old woman, who went and told Riel that we had arrived and wished to speak with him. He left the chapel and when I saw him I advanced with my hand out. He took it and said, "You are plainly a man who has travelled far. Though you seem to know me, I don't know you."

"Yes, I know you," I answered. "Every Métis knows the name Louis Riel. And you may remember me. Do you recognize the name Gabriel Dumont?"

"Of course," he answered. "I know that name well. It has been many years, and it is good see you again. But please, you must excuse me. I must return to hear the rest of the Mass. Please wait for me at my house, over there near the bridge. My wife will welcome you, and I will join you as quickly as I can."

When the Mass had finished he asked why we had come. He appeared surprised and flattered by our request. I will always remember his words:

God wants you to understand that you are following the right track, because there are four of you and you have arrived on the fourth. Since you wish to leave with a fifth, I can not answer you today. You must wait until the fifth to hear my decision.

The next morning Riel said: "Fifteen years ago I gave my heart to my people. I am ready to give it again now, but I can not leave my small family. If you will arrange for them to accompany me, I will go with you. Also, I can not leave for eight days. I am employed as a teacher here, and the Métis children here need a teacher—I must make proper arrangements before I can leave."

So eight days later we set off. When we reached Fort Benton, Riel took Mass, as he always did when near a church. Then he went to the priest to ask his blessing. At first the priest refused. The next morning Riel went to Mass again, and when he was leaving the priest said, "Yesterday I refused because I didn't think my blessing would be of any use to you. But I see you still want it, so I will give it to you now."

I joined Riel to receive the priest's blessing; Jimmie, Moïse, and Dumas did not think it was important. Riel and I kneeled together at the communion table. Immediately after we received the blessing, the priest came to see us off and found Riel staring at the crest of a nearby hill. "Father," he said, "I see a gallows on that hill, and I am swinging from it."

As we travelled I suddenly found myself reciting a little prayer: "Father, give me courage, and belief, and faith in the blessing I received in Your sacred name, so that I will remember this moment until the hour of my death. Amen." Riel liked it, and often asked me repeat it for him. Every day since then, and any time that I wanted to encourage myself, I have recited my little prayer. It came from the deepest heart of me, from a small moment when I knew for a certainty that Louis Riel saw farther into the future than I did.

Three weeks after we left Saint Peter's Mission we reached Fish Creek. Sixty Métis hunters waited to greet us. They fired their rifles and shouted with joy, and this night we stayed at Gabriel's Crossing, some in the house and the rest in tents. Madeleine made sure everyone was fed; she was particularly attentive to Madame Riel and her children.

Charles Nolin was there too, with his huge, sagging, split face—always seeming about to laugh and weep at the same time. I do not often misread people, but Nolin had convinced me that since he had moved to the Saskatchewan he had been working honestly for the Métis. He was Riel's cousin, but had turned against him in 1869. One remarkable thing about Riel: he harboured no bitterness. When I said Nolin was reliable, Riel accepted my word.

Next day I rode ahead to Batoche to ask Father Moulin to open the church so Riel could make a speech there. But so many people wanted to hear him that the church was too small. Riel spoke outside, under the great tent of the sky. He spoke of treaties and the things in our Bill of Rights.

To the Métis People of the St. Laurent Commune:

Usually when visitors enter the dwelling of a very poor man, they experience a painful feeling. But on entering M. Riel's house, our impression was very different. His humble home reminded us of the times in years past when he had the opportunity to enrich himself and indeed to make a considerable fortune; it also reminded us how completely, despite everything, he was committed to his nation. We know how he worked for Manitoba and how he struggled on behalf of everyone in the North West, and having seen how little he had worked for his own benefit, we have returned, after a long journey of almost fourteen hundred miles, with double the confidence we had when we left to seek him out in that strange land.

GABRIEL DUMONT

MOÏSE OULETTE

MICHEL DUMAS

JAMES IBISTER

Just before the battle at Duck Lake my brother Isidore and Albert Monkman both said, "Exovede, you came for our rights, but now you speak only of religion. If we fight, it is not for your religion but for our rights." And Riel replied, "Be careful, my brothers. Don't you realize that my religion and your rights are the same?"

Riel affected people in strange ways. Some days after the Battle at Fish Creek, he and Albert Monkman led fifty men to Duck Lake to scout the country. On his return, Riel said to me, "The man commanding our troops on the other side of the river plans to betray us. He urges two of your men to abandon us. Please go over and tell him that I know what he has in mind."

I crossed the river and asked my men if anyone was urging them to desert. No one would answer. So Riel crossed with me and collected them all together. "My friends," he said, "I know that someone urges you to betray us. You refuse to reveal who that man is to M. Dumont, but rest assured that I know who the guilty man is, and even if we must execute him, you will all learn the truth."

Patrice Fleury then said, "It is true. Monkman suggested that I desert." Garçon Belanger said the same thing.

I had Monkman escorted to Batoche under guard. With Patrice and Garçon as witnesses against him, before the council I asked Monkman to answer the accusation against him.

"It is true," he said. "I have no intention of deserting, but I *had* to find out if Riel has second sight."

FATHER ALEXIS ANDRÉ, *priest*

Albert Monkman is a man who has been very much, and very unfairly, abused and maligned. I always found him kind and good, and he always took the side of the weak and defenseless against Riel, to his own very great danger and risk. Although he was not a Catholic himself, I believe that he prevented the burning of the Catholic churches at Duck Lake and St. Laurent. Riel had him imprisoned because Monkman opposed him in every way he could.

Once, when I was young, I came upon a warrior on the prairie. We rode hard at each other, each certain that the other would turn away first. When I got near enough I recognized he was a Blood. He turned first. He was armed, but our meeting was so unexpected that he had no time to draw an arrow from his quiver. Since he could not fight, I did not want to hurt him, just unsaddle him.

Now our horses are shoulder to shoulder. The Blood will not stop. I am right beside him, so I pull up on my reins and jump on his horse behind him. I grab both his arms so he can not defend himself and take him back to my camp. I give him a pipe of tobacco, which he smokes without getting off his horse. When I tell him he can go, he leaves as fast as his horse can carry him.

That was a simple case of my courage against his, and mine won out. Louis Riel brought much more than simple courage to our battles. He was inspired—a visionary. At times he could see into the future. About a month after we arrived at St. Laurent in 1884, he began explaining the ancient history of the Métis people to me. He showed me a letter that Bishop Ignace Bourget had written describing his divine mission, and a book called *The Prophecies of St. Bridget* that was written in buffalo blood.

Montreal, July 14, 1875

Dear Mister Riel,
I received your letter of July 6 yesterday and I was greatly touched, for that letter proves to me that you are animated by good motives and, at the same time, tormented in your mind by other inclinations or by something which I do not understand, which makes you undecided about carrying out the duties imposed on you by the obedience in which you live.

So I have the intimate conviction that you will receive in this world, and sooner than you think, the reward for all those mental and moral sacrifices you make, which are a thousand times more crushing than the sacrifices of material and visible life.

God, who has always led you and assisted you until the present hour, will not abandon you in the dark hours of your life, for he has given you a mission which you must fulfill in all respects.

By the Grace of God, you will persevere in the way which has been traced out for you. This is to say, you must not withhold anything you possess. You will desire above all things to know God and to procure the greatest glory for Him. You will work unceasingly for the honour of religion, the salvation of souls, and the good of society. And you will sanctify yourself in desiring heartily the sanctification of others.

Yours in the Love of God,

BISHOP IGNACE BOURGET

Some moments in life stay with you. Because you are totally alive in them, they ring true. In my mind I can see the bloody letters of *The Prophecies of Saint Bridget.* I can still hear Riel's words as he told me our history:

The Spirit of God came to me as it appeared to Moses, in the midst of clouds of flame. I was astonished. I was dumbfounded. It spoke to me and said:

"Rise. You will go; you will find; you will say Saint Ignace Bourget has you. Fall to your knees and implore him. Say God has anointed you, with His divine gifts and the fruits of His Spirit, as the prophet of the New World. You are called to regenerate the world. You are a divine bull. Bellow your faith to the world, so it hears your prophecies.

"You are not only Louis Riel, but also David Mordecai, a Jew. You, David Mordecai, were born in Marseille, France, into the house of Lazarus. You came to North America as a child, and your similarity to Louis Riel is so great that you were as identical as twins. When you died in the Mississippi

River your spirit infused Louis Riel. Even those in charge of him did not detect the change. You are the new Saviour, sent to succour all Jews and Gentiles from their bondage.

"King David was seven-eighths Jewish and one-eighth Gentile (through his Moabite great-grandmother Ruth). You, Louis 'David' Riel are seven-eighths French-Canadian and one-eighth Chipewyan. You must re-establish the people dear to me."

On December 14, 1875, at one o'clock in the afternoon, the Spirit of God came upon me again, and filled my body and soul with His divine essence. It transported me to the fourth heaven and instructed me about the nations of the earth:

"The Indians of the northern part of this continent are of Jewish origin.

"The Indians of the south of this continent are Egyptians.

"At the moment the infant Moses was discovered floating on the Nile, an Egyptian ship went astray in the Atlantic. Forty-four people were aboard, twenty-seven Egyptians and three families of Hebrew slaves. The Egyptians numbered twenty-two men and five women. The Hebrew families were led by Ihami of the tribe of Zabulon; Agareon, also of Zabulon; and Omorug of the tribe of Reuben.

"For a year and a half the ship wandered aimlessly off course, until Agareon sacrificed bread and wine to the God of his fathers. 'O God of Abraham, Isaac, and Jacob,' he prayed, 'Do not take from my children the land you have promised them.' 'Father,' said his little daughter when she heard his words, 'you always look back. But we must sail toward the great orange sun.' Nineteen days later the ship reached America.

"That lost ship discovered this continent.

"The Egyptians despised the Hebrews, but feared them because God had answered Agareon's prayers. So they released them from their slavery and drove them off into the wilderness, keeping only some of their daughters as wives.

"The Egyptians, with their knowledge of civilization, created the empires of Montezuma and of Peru. But the uneducated Hebrews, newly emerged from oppression, could only lead a very primitive and simple life.

"The Egyptians were the fathers of the great Indian empires of South America. The Hebrews populated North America, and the Indian and Métis people are their descendants."

Then the Spirit of God took hold of me, and fixed my gaze on a vision of the chair of the Pope. As the Lord desired, I measured the length of the chair. It was twenty-three feet, three inches, and three lines long. The feet are centuries; the inches are epochs of ten years; the lines are years. God spoke to me again:

"The First Cycle lasted 2333 years. The Mission of Ezra, the Jewish preparation, lasted 457 years—until the birth of Christ; the Roman fulfillment has lasted 1876 years; a total of 2333 years. The Second Cycle, the Religion in the New World, shall also last 2333 years: the French-Canadian preparation shall last 457 years; and the Métis fulfillment 1876 years. Then shall come the Parousia, and the Kingdom of Heaven on this earth.

"You will bring in immigrants from all the Catholic countries of Europe—Ireland, Italy, Poland, Bavaria—and encourage them to marry Indian women. Thus, the entire Indian race of North America will give way to a new race: a race of Métis of different fatherlands. And these new Métis nations will create a religious system of universal harmony."

And the voice of God rang out:

"In My hands the earth is no bigger than an egg. If I want to destroy it, I have only to let it fall into space. But I will not abandon it. I will care for it, hold it. Now I only shake it. For by shaking it near My ear, I can hear its inner noises and feel its volcanic fire. Do not fear volcanoes, not even the most terrible eruptions. It is I who do it all. I amuse myself with the points of My crown and pierce the shell of the egg. With one flick of My thumb, I can make your hills bend like the back of a bull when he struggles to his feet, roused by a kick from the herdsman. I will protect you."

Two months after Riel returned with us from Montana the Canadian Government could have shown us its good faith. Ottawa sent us a message saying that the Minister of Public Works intended to come to the North-West Territories, and that he would visit Batoche to speak with us. Despite our poor harvest and a bad hunting season, we organized a feast. Riel wrote a speech. We set up tables in the meadow behind the church, hung banners, and called the best fiddlers from all the nearby villages to a great dance. A bunch of us rode out to greet the Minister on the road, as if he were Lord Lorne or the Prime Minister himself, but he didn't arrive. We sent scouts, hoping that he had not had trouble. We waited a day and a night, then began returning to our farms. This big Government chief never bothered to tell us that he had changed his plans. We were humiliated. We offered the best we had, and this Minister and his Government shit in our pots. After that we believed nothing they said. I think they planned to send their soldiers against us from the beginning. They wanted our land, and nothing we did would stop them from taking it.

The Métis are a distinct people, and the French-Canadians who move to the North West must identify with us and accept our new nation. Then God will drive from our path all troublesome priests who do not acknowledge our divine mission.

We needed the priests' help. In September 1884, Bishop Grandin came to Batoche with Father André, Father Vegreville, and Amédée Forget to meet with us. I spoke to them. I asked why they refused to help us, why they deliberately stayed away from our meetings. Their absence made us uneasy. I reminded Father André of 1875 and of the St. Laurent commune he had suggested we form. All we wanted were our rights.

Riel closed that meeting by suggesting to Bishop Grandin that he grant us a saintly protector and a special national feast day, so we would be like the French-Canadians with their feast of St. Jean-Baptiste. Riel suggested St. Joseph, father of Our Lord the Christ. Bishop Grandin agreed and said that July 24 would be a good day for our national feast. We decided to celebrate our first national day early, because July 24 had passed already and we did not want to wait for another year to pass. We planned a festival for September 24.

Later this day I spoke privately with Bishop Grandin. I said that the priests had abandoned us. Then I went to visit Forget, who was staying with Joseph Vandal, who had a house near Gabriel's Crossing. I gave Forget a written copy of our demands and told him how frustrated we all were with the Government. At the time I thought he was our friend, but now I know that he came as a spy.

AMÉDÉE FORGET, *to Lieutenant Governor Dewdney*

We proceeded to Gabriel Dumont's crossing and stopped the night of September 6, 1884 with Mister Joseph Vandal. Mister Dumont called during the evening and addressed me substantially as follows:

"You are an officer of the government but you are also our friend, and will, I am sure, help us with the Governor. The Government has ignored our rights and looks down upon us with contempt. Not having anyone among us capable of speaking and writing for us, we went for Mister Riel. Before leaving we were told that we and he would be arrested. We don't believe that the Government should try to touch any one of us so long as we don't do anything wrong. If they try, the consequences will be on them. Mister Riel is now with us and we will see to his personal safety. He is a political leader, but in other matters I am the chief here.

"I want also to speak about the Indians. They are our relatives; when they are starving they come to us for relief and we have to feed them. I was present at the treaty. I don't know the words on the paper they signed; but everyone there understood that not only would they live as well as they had before, but better. Is that what is taking place now? They are starving. The Government does not do right by them. We want the

Indians fed, our rights recognized, and Mister Riel as our leader; we don't want to create any disturbance. We do not have violence on our minds.

"I am certain that if we cool-headed Métis had to face the dilemma of renouncing our rights or winning them by bloodshed, there is not one of us who would not make a joke of it by saying: 'Keep your rights! If we have to die for them, we can do without them after all!'"

Last nights of the Hunter's Moon and the leaves whisper like thoughts. I tread my past underfoot, a sloppy, purpling carpet of memories. Face it! The wrinkles on a forehead are battle scars. Reckonings aplenty lie there. The Canadians have left a lot of emotion raging loose, without legitimate employment.

JOHN DONKIN, *policeman*

Shortly before Christmas I visited the store at Dumont's Crossing. It was a simple shack about fourteen foot square, and smack in the middle of it sat a fine slate billiard table covered in blue-green velvet. It looked to me almost like a summer pond in that drab wintery country. It must have been expensive to ship in from the east, and was Dumont's pride and joy. Inside the store the air was foggy with smoke. I recall the click of ivory, and a long argument over the finer rules of French Billiards. Dumont was the unquestioned champion, really quite adept at the game. The habitués were imbibing a nauseous hop-beer, and talked much violent sedition.

During the rebellion the soldiers stole that billiard table, and afterwards Dumont petitioned the government for its return. He never got it back.

On New Year's day 1885 we held the feast we had organized for the Government Minister, with Louis Riel as our guest of honour. Madeleine and a few other women made a new dress for Madame Riel, and we all danced and celebrated. A group from Charles Nolin's village read a letter:

> We will not allow this opportunity to pass without recognizing the respect, gratitude, and affection that all the French persons living in the North West Territories feel for the man we regard as the true Father of Manitoba. To us you are a Roman, a valiant chief who will bring us justice. You are the father who puts our interests before his own. .

Charles Nolin—his great sagging face. He could be noble but not often. Riel was his cousin but they were not similar. Nolin lied at the trial when he said Riel came to the Saskatchewan only in search of money. He spoke, as always, only about what he wanted for himself.

At first Nolin was a leader. And after they reconciled and Riel stayed with him, a miracle happened in his house. For ten years his wife Rosalie had suffered. Nolin had tried everything to heal her. In December he begged some sacred Lourdes water from the nuns at Batoche, and all his relatives attended the novena he held for Rosalie, and when the youngest child patted the water onto her limbs, Rosalie cried out, said she burned. Then her weakness disappeared and she was healed. For ten years Nolin had prayed for a cure. It only happened after Riel forgave him for betraying the Métis in 1869.

In January Riel and I asked Nolin to support our demands, to reject the contract that the Government had awarded him to construct the telegraph line between Edmonton and Duck Lake. "I will do this," he said, "only if Louis will represent us on the North West Council and abandon his plan of returning to Montana." "I agree to this," said Riel.

Riel owned almost nothing. This cane I now carry is one of the few things that belonged to him. It came from Mexico and was carved by our Mestizo brothers there. A friend of the Métis gave it to Riel when he was in Montana. He saw it as an emblem of our greater struggle, of the struggle of all the native peoples. When he gave it to me as a gesture of friendship, I offered him my absolute loyalty in return.

PHILIPPE GARNOT, *Secretary to the Exovedate*

Let me tell you about Charles Nolin. Charles Nolin is a devious man, emotionally incapable of dealing openly or honestly with people. He is ambitious and ignorant and, worst of all, an egoist who is absolutely unconcerned about ruining other people if that serves to advance him. He came to St. Laurent having disgraced himself in Manitoba, and immediately began scheming to manipulate people here. Gabriel Dumont suited Nolin's needs because Gabriel had a great deal of influence among the Métis in Saskatchewan. Nolin treated Gabriel like a brother, and so began to manipulate the whole community—though in fairness to him I feel I must do Nolin the justice of believing that he did not have *any* idea how catastrophic his machinations would be.

I recall one speech Nolin made that clearly indicated the direction in which he was pushing us. "God," he said, "sometimes uses very small things to punish powerful nations: cutworms and grasshoppers destroy their harvest, for instance, and humble them. Maybe it is the intention of Divine Providence to employ our small Métis nation to punish the English for their pride and injustice."

Gabriel was flattered by Nolin's attention and, because he was a frank and generous man, Nolin had no difficulty manipulating him. Yet I must give credit to Gabriel's many fine qualities, too. Had he been educated, I am convinced that his education would undoubtedly have united with his innate intelligence to produce a brilliant man. And there is no doubt in my mind that he wished to serve the Métis cause any way he could.

Still, Gabriel is not without his own egotistical defects. Though he has achieved a great reputation for bravery, the world must not accept that he is as valiant as he would have it believe. His bravery is like the bravery of an Indian who exposes himself to the greatest possible danger for a few instants and then withdraws, believing that by this action he deserves recognition for bravery. That is not bravery but lunacy in my view, because risking your life like that does nothing for the community.

Riel was furious when the Government telegram from Dewdney in February 1885 came to Charles Nolin offering a Commission to discuss our grievances. It came to *Nolin*, not Riel or me who were the leaders. I had come to expect humiliation from the Canadians, but Riel said, "Four hundred years ago the English began their robbing. Now we put a stop to it. In forty days, Ottawa will have our answer."

When the police embarrassed the St. Laurent colony in 1875, I had accepted Canadian authority, but I could not accept it any longer. By 1885, the Indians were starving, and I knew that if we didn't do something quickly, before too many years had passed the Métis would starve too. Now I was prepared to fight.

Life is not what it was when I was a young man proving myself against the Indians, and total war is a desperate enterprise. What did I have to gain by going to war? I had a house and a family, and was not starving nor cold. Whatever you have been told or may believe, I didn't want to go to war. But when my people spoke, we were ignored. The politicians in Ottawa didn't respect us. Canada stole from us, and from the Indians, and from all the peoples of the North-West. Other than fighting, our only choice was to watch Canada take our children's future from them.

One morning Riel said to me, "Uncle Gabriel, I had a dream. I saw a flock of dark geese. They seemed to rise on the wind, but really hung immobile in the sky. I saw them divided, as if in two groups. The leading goose suddenly turned and flew west. The other geese were in the sunlight, but didn't reflect it. They were covered with shadow. If you warriors fight for evil motives, you are like the dark geese. God will stop you in mid-flight. You will lose your way. Hear, pay attention, obey, and you will escape the setbacks, the defeats, and the shame that drag you low. The Métis must not be the geese. We must not divide."

Once again he had looked into the future. But I must say that had we fought as I wanted, fewer of my people and more of the English would have died. I regret that we didn't fight like the warriors we were. Although we hoped that Riel could convince the Canadians to listen, by March I knew that war was our only option. With the men in whom I had most confidence—my brother Isidore, my cousin Augustin, Napoléon Nault, and some other hunters—I signed the oath of revolution that Riel drew up for us. We had been forced into war. I wanted it in writing so the future would know that we were honest men.

It was morning. We took the oath to Charles Nolin to sign. He spoke constantly to the priests by this time, so we wanted his promise that he was with us. He refused to sign. He asked us to take a novena, during which every Métis would fast and pray. He said that the Government would send emissaries to meet with us at the end of this time. We were not yet ready, and it is always a good thing to think before you fight, so Riel and I agreed. We arranged to end the novena on St. Joseph of the Métis Day, when the whole nation came together.

The Oath of Revolution

We, the undersigned, pledge ourselves deliberately and voluntarily to do everything we can to:

1. Save our souls by trying day and night to live a holy life everywhere and in all respects.
2. Save our country from a wicked Government by taking up arms if necessary.

May God the almighty Father help us. Jesus, Mary, Joseph, Saint John the Baptist, intercede for us! Pray for us unceasingly, so that we may gain your successes, your victories, your triumphs, for ever and ever; for these are the successes, victories, and triumphs of God Himself.

We particularly pledge ourselves to raise our families in a holy way and to ceaselessly practise the greatest trust in God; in Jesus, Mary, Joseph, and Saint John the Baptist; and in all our patron saints. For our banner we take the commandments of God, and the Church, and the inspiring cross of Jesus Christ our Lord.

JOSEPH OULLETTE

GABRIEL DUMONT

PIERRE GARIÉPUY

ISIDORE DUMONT

JOHN ROSS

PHILIPPE GARIÉPUY

AUGUSTE LAFRAMBOISE

MOÏSE OUELLETTE

CALIXTE LAFONTAINE

NAPOLÉON NAULT

More promises from the Government would not have satisfied us. During one public meeting, Riel had said: "Surely they must answer us at least yes or no. We only ask for what they have already promised us. They can not say no. If they won't recognize our rights, we must rebel again."

After this, the word *rebellion* was on the tongue of every Métis. We recognized how serious it was, but you must realize that rebellion did not have the tragic implications then that it has now. We all remembered 1870 as having really been a very peaceful rebellion. The only victim, Scott, brought on his own fate with his fanaticism. So those Métis who spoke openly about rebellion believed that a little bit of clamouring and threatening would bring us our rights. They did not have bloodshed on their minds. Deep in their hearts, no people in the world are as strong and patient and good as the Métis. Given a choice between wealth and justice, we will always choose justice. Not one of our petitions was answered, and we had all lost patience, but we honestly believed that everything would work out peacefully in the end.

Still, when Riel made his statement about rebellion, I acted swiftly. While the others took the novena and prayed, I rode out among the Indians, asking them to honour the tobacco they had smoked with my family and me. I asked them to stand by the Métis, as the Métis always stood by them in their times of need. Beardy agreed, but One Arrow hesitated. I reminded him of the covenants of honour.

One day before our festival to celebrate St. Joseph de Métis I stopped at the Touronds' farm, where only a few months earlier we had gathered to greet Riel. This night I rode on to sleep in my own bed. Madeleine cooked me a fine dinner, and after dinner we went outside. When I looked at her face, it was green.

"Madeleine," I said, "are you ill? You look green." "No," she said. "Your face is green, too." We looked at the sky and just at dusk there was an eclipse of the sun.

Riel intended to join us the next morning for our parade to Batoche. Doctor John Willoughby had a store near the Touronds' farm, and the Touronds told me that Willoughby and Norbert Welsh had arrived there. Because Welsh was not trustworthy—he had always sided with the Hudson's Bay Company—I suspected that they were probably spies for the police. However, Welsh had once been a buffalo hunter. We had that in common, and I thought I might learn something from him.

In the morning I met Welsh and Willoughby on the road. I told Welsh that if he wanted to speak to Riel, he should attend our meeting at Baptiste Rochelle's home. I got there first. There was a thick stand of poplar trees screening Rochelle's house. The house had a lot of big windows, and as Welsh and Willoughby drew near I saw them. I went outside. Welsh was nervous and very aggressive. He put the lash to his mare, nearly driving her through the open door into the house. I seized the reins and ordered them out of their sleigh. Welsh was sarcastic and afraid. I had my foster son Alexi unhitch the horse and put it in the stable—I didn't want them to escape before we could determine exactly why they had come.

When I led them into the house, Riel began to pace back and forth. He ignored Welsh, but was very curious about Willoughby. Finally he said, "The time has come when men must choose whether or not they have lived a good life." Then he asked Willoughby his name and which church he belonged to.

Willoughby turned pale and answered that he was Presbyterian. "Of the root of the Devil," said Riel with a smile. "But I feel you are a good-hearted, charitable man. There is a difference between Protestantism and Orangism. Protestantism is a branch on the tree of true religion. Do you understand that the time has come for the Métis nation to strike a blow for their rights?"

Willoughby said that he understood, and that the white colonists had some grievances of their own, but they chose to resolve them differently. Riel answered that he more than anyone knew the grievances of the white colonists: the Métis had addressed many petitions to the Government on everyone's behalf, and the only answer we had received was more policemen in the country.

"But now we have our own police force," Riel said, nodding toward me and my men. "In a week we could exterminate that pathetic Government force, but you colonists are our neighbours, and we don't wish to put you at risk.

"I sent a proclamation to Pembina. As soon as it goes out, all the Métis and Indians in the United States will be at my back. The time has come when the Métis must govern the country or perish. I have called on all the great Catholic nations, the Irishmen and Germans, the Italians, Bavarians, and Poles, to come to our aid. When we obtain our rights and divide the North-West Territories, we will divide the land in seven parts, and give a different one to each of our allies."

Riel then turned to Welsh and said, "Welsh, eh? I must know your name in full."

Welsh drew a letter from his pocket and said, "There are my name and address in full."

Riel read the letter and said, "This tells me you are not a true Métis. You have one week to pray and face your God."

Riel then left them and called me to a corner of the room. "You can let them go," he said. "They are not spies. If we need them, we will pick them up later."

This same day, Lawrence Clarke, that great friend to the Métis, returned from Winnipeg through Qu'Appelle. When he passed through Batoche, Clarke asked Michel Dumas and Napoléon Nault, "Are you still holding all those meetings? Did the Government answer your petitions?"

Dumas answered, "Yes. We hold meetings nearly every day now."

"Fine," said Clarke. "Good! You won't hold them very much longer. There are eighty soldiers on the way. I saw them at Humboldt, and tomorrow or the next day they will arrest Riel and Dumont. You threaten the Government with petitions. We will send you bullets in return."

Naturally everyone was excited. Next afternoon we had a general meeting at the church. Riel and I addressed the crowd. I said, "The police intend to take Riel. What are you going to do? Here is a man who has done so much for us. Will you let them take him from us? We must make a plan."

Riel then said, "We send petitions; they send the police to imprison Gabriel Dumont and me. But I know what went wrong: *I* was the mistake. The Government hates me because I forced it to negotiate once. Because I am here you will get nothing. I must leave, and it must be now. When I go the Government may acknowledge your rights. Yes. I think it is time I went back to Montana."

The meeting exploded. "No!" they cried. "We won't let you go. You have worked so very hard for our rights. You can not quit now."

Riel said, "If you won't permit me to go freely, I must desert you."

One ancient Métis hunter stood and said, "Nephew, you are our hope. If you abandon us, we will follow you. We will move to Montana with you, and leave this country of ours behind."

I said, "I think that our Uncle Louis is talking sense. We must cross the line. In Montana, we won't be insulted or taken prisoner."

"No!" roared the crowd. "We won't allow it. Do not be afraid of being taken prisoner."

"What are you saying?" I asked them.

"We will take arms when they come," they shouted. "No one will lay a hand on either of you."

"Do you understand what you are saying?" I asked. "You speak as if you want to fight, but what weapons do you have for fighting a Government? How determined are you to stand fast?"

They shouted, "If we must, we *will* fight."

Riel was still not prepared to say that he would stay with us, so I continued to speak. I shouted, "'Yes!' you say. I know you all very well. I know you as if you were my children. I know how resolute you are. It is good to be resolute, but I ask you again: How many of you will fight with me?"

Instead of raising their hands, the whole crowd rose and howled: "If the time has come to die for our country, we will all die together."

I stood frozen and astonished. I was the most ardent one there and had proven many times that I was not afraid to fight, but I tried to remain calm. I tried to make them see that they had to think carefully about this. I said, "I see that you have decided. But I ask again: Will you grow tired and discouraged? If I start this fight, I will not stop until we win. How many of you will be with me at the end? Two? Three?"

"We will all fight with you until the end," they shouted.

"Good!" I cried. "This is very, very good. If you are determined to fight, I will lead you."

"Yes!" they cried. "Lead us. To arms! To arms!"

These are the facts. This is the way our fight began. Without the news from Clarke that the police intended to take Riel, no one would have dreamed of taking up arms. It was Clarke who put spark to the powder. Until that moment, no one had seriously considered an armed rebellion. It might eventually have come to that, but by then all peaceful means would have been exhausted. Fighting was our last option. And the tragedy is that Clarke was just lying to frighten us; but we had already been pushed to the edge.

As we left the meeting Riel said to me, "If this turns bad and we leaders are captured, many of our followers will be lost. We must remember that."

4

Memories whirl down from the sky. They cling like fat snowflakes.
Father, give me courage, and belief, and faith in the sacred blessing I
received in Your name.

Knowing that the police were on their way to arrest Riel and me, we rode in a group to Batoche to celebrate the end of Nolin's novena. We stopped at Kerr's store to take what weapons we could find. When we reached St. Anthony of Padua church, which my men and I had built with our own hands, the traitorous priest Moulin said, "I protest. You will not use this church to oppose authority."

"Look at this," cried Riel. "Another Protestant." We laughed Moulin aside and threw open the doors of our church.

Riel stood near the altar and all the hunters crowded around him. "Rome has fallen!" he cried. "When I first entered your church I stood at the back with my head bowed. Every time after that, you nudged me a little closer, until here I am today. But who brought me to the altar? The Good Lord. Who speaks from my mouth when I speak to you? It is God. Does anyone want me to touch the altar to prove my powers? No? Another time then. Now let us celebrate the arrival of Jesus at Jerusalem."

He sang and the hunters danced around him clamouring with joy. He breathed on us, filling us with the Holy Spirit. "The tyrannical papists are no longer your masters," he cried. "Priests have too many books for true religion. *St. Bridget* and the Bible are enough for us."

Quand je vous parle, c'est la voix de Dieu qui sonne
Et tout ce que je dis vous est essentiel.
Je suis le joyeux téléphone
Qui vous transmet les chants et les discours du ciel.

When I speak to you, it is the voice of God that speaks
And all that I tell you is inspired.
I am the joyous telephone
That transmits the songs and words of the sky to you.

Quand je vous parle, c'est la voix de Dieu qui sonne
Et tout ce que je dis vous est essentiel.
Je suis le joyeux téléphone

When I speak to you, it is the voice of God that speaks
And everything I say to you is inspired.
I am the joyous telephone.

LOUIS "DAVID" RIEL

Night had fallen by then, and the whole Métis nation voted unanimously to support the provisional government. Riel called the high council the Exovedate, because they were the chosen from the Métis flock. Louison Batoche had disappeared from the village, so we installed our command post in his house.

We were sure that the Canadians could not attack us immediately because Riel had learned that the English Government had declared war on Russia. Canada could not expect assistance from England. Nevertheless, we threw ourselves into our preparations. I organized the army. Then we sent for Louis Marion,

Baptiste Boyer, and Charles Nolin, who had all refused to fight with us. Nolin was the guiltiest, because he had been a voice for rebellion all along. We remembered his actions during the rebellion in 1869, and Riel decided to try him for treason to the nation. He recommended the death penalty.

Not many men can master their fear, and Nolin was terrified. He begged us for mercy. But we didn't intend to condemn him to death. Instead we established him as Commissar for the nation, so now he had the title he had always wanted. "There, Charles Nolin," I said. "Now I think the Métis cart has wheels enough to go forward. You can no longer unbalance us by running to the English and saying that you are innocent of all involvement."

The Exovedate met every day. The other chiefs had to understand, as I did, the reasons for taking arms and how history had put God and justice on our side. We all had to accept the strategy Riel wanted to employ, which was what I found most difficult. He began to organize our religion, and the Exovedate accepted him as prophet to the Métis people.

To All the Métis People
The French Canadian Métis Exovedate recognizes Louis "David" Riel as a prophet in the service of Jesus Christ the son of God and the only Redeemer of the world; as a prophet at the feet of Mary Immaculate under the powerful and most favourable protection of the Virgin Mother of Christ; as a

prophet under the visible and most comforting protection of Saint Joseph, the chosen patron of the Métis, the patron of the universal church; as a prophet humbly imitating in many ways Saint John the Baptiste, the glorious patron of the French Canadians and the French-Canadian Métis.

The Exovedate decrees:

That the commandments of God be the laws of the Provisional Government. That we recognize the right of Monsieur Louis "David" Riel to direct the priests. That Archbishop Ignace Bourget is recognized from today by the French-Canadian people of the Saskatchewan as the pope of the New World.

The Exovedate decrees:

That Hell will not last forever. Such doctrine is contrary to divine mercy. Even if it be prolonged for millions and millions of years, a sentence in Hell must one day come to an end.

One thing: although Riel was a great man, I did not always agree with how he led our people; still, he listened to me when I advised him. Once, after we pressured Philippe Garnot to become Secretary of the Exovedate, Riel tried to get him to fight too. But Garnot did not want to fight, and I did not want soldiers who did not want to fight. Riel tried to humiliate Garnot into fighting. Finally I stood up before the Council and said that anyone who was not prepared to take up arms freely and of their own will should not be allowed to fight. I said that Garnot was doing valuable work for us, and he should not have to fight if he did not want to. And that was that.

Batoche, N.W.T.

Saint Joseph de Métis, 1898

Dear M. Trémaudan

Thank you for your recent letter. I have spoken with
Gabriel Dumont, but he refuses to correspond with you. He
said that he told the whole history to M. Demanche, and he is
fed up with talking.

However, if you are interested I have a few observations of
my own to offer. Toward the end of the rebellion, Riel was the
problem, not Gabriel. It was disgusting to see a man with
Riel's cleverness impose his influence on superstitious and
ignorant people. He convinced them that he was a prophet:
they even passed a resolution in the Council recognizing him
as prophet by the grace of God. Every morning he appeared
before the Council and delivered his prophecies. He always
began with these words: "The Spirit of God told me" or "The
Spirit of God made me see." The majority had such a faith in
his prophecies that they would have flung themselves into the
Saskatchewan River if "The Spirit of God" had told Riel they
must.

I doubt if there were ten persons in Batoche who didn't
believe him, and these persons didn't dare say it. To give you
an idea of how he used his influence, I am going to describe an
incident that took place between him and me. Part of it
happened before the Council and the remainder behind the
stage.

He asked me one day why I persisted to refuse to take arms.
I explained to him that I could not fight against my compa-
triots, parents, or friends who had taken arms against us; but at
the same time I pointed to my carbine, which was in my house
where the sessions of Council took place, saying that I was
prepared to protect my house against whomever might feel

disposed to attack it. In fact I had shown four Sioux to the door a little brusquely that same evening. But Riel continued to torment me, trying to force me to say that I was prepared to become a soldier in order to encourage some English Métis who were there to follow my example. But I succeeded in making my point well enough to keep the Council on my side, and he was forced to back down. Gabriel, who followed Riel in most cases, abandoned him and was on my side that evening.

Riel asked then that I review the guards with him. I accepted and followed him. But instead of going toward the first sentry, who was on the road near the forge, he led me out behind the houses and told me that he wished to speak privately to me. I am going to repeat what he said to me, as clearly as I can recall it. "Garnot," he said, "you make me very angry and I even have some suspicions about you. You probably know that if you had not agreed to be our secretary at the beginning of this affair we would have punished you. You also know that every word you say against me or the religion that I am trying to reform causes me trouble, and that you can not do or say anything without the Spirit of God warning me of your intention."

I began to laugh. He was a little insulted and left me for a time. Then he returned to ask, "Why do you laugh? Do you doubt my words?" I said, "No. But if in the place of the Spirit of God you said that the words of Damase Carrière warned you of my intentions, I might be capable of choking off my laughter." Riel began to praise Damase Carrière and finished by telling me that it was Damase Carrière who had reported everything to him. He concluded, however, by saying, "I give you carte blanche under the covenants of the religion, but it is necessary that you keep silent from now on and not share your observations with people." I promised and kept my promise.

Poor Damase Carrière. The English mistook him for Riel. They looped a rope around his neck and dragged him behind a horse until the life was choked out of him. The rebellion was a great tragedy for all of us.

Respectfully yours,

PHILIPPE GARNOT

Soon after we took up arms, I had my men cut the telegraph lines and we began to take prisoners. As Napoléon Nault and I rode out one cold morning toward Fish Creek, the Indian agent and his man approached us. The Indian agent had always been good-hearted to the Indians. I said, "You are now my prisoners."

"Why?" he asked.

"The Métis have decided to stand up to Government injustice," I said, "and I am taking everyone prisoner who works for the Government."

"Good," said the Indian agent. "I am in favour of this. Take us."

A little farther down the track a Red River cart came squealing toward us. A man named Jardine drove it, and when he saw me coming he whipped his horses. "Stop!" I shouted, "or I will kill your horses." He stopped.

I asked, "Where are you going?"

"That is none of your affair," he said.

"Then it must not be an honest trip," I said. "I think you ride to Duck Lake to tell the police what has happened. You are my prisoner."

"But what about my horses?" he asked.

I laughed out loud. "What a strange thing to ask. They are also my prisoners, of course."

"Honestly," said Jardine, "I have just gotten medicine for my sick wife and I must get it to her."

"Give it to me then, and I will see that she gets it," I said. I handed it to one of my young men. "See. Here, I am sending a man to take it to her immediately. Now come with us."

This same evening Isidore and Augustin captured the two men who tried to repair the telegraph line. When they arrived at Batoche I met them. "Have you disarmed them?" I asked. "No," they said. "Fine captains you are," I told them. But you see how unprepared most of us were for war. I searched the prisoners myself. They were not carrying any weapons.

The year Madeleine married me, in the spring, Isidore, Augustin, Edouard, Damase Carrière, and Louis Marion said, "Gabriel, we must go for one last free hunt. Soon Madeleine will have you, and you won't have time for us." We told everyone that we were going after Cabree, but really we only wanted to be together.

It was strange hunting, because we remained close together the whole time. Whenever one of us suggested something, we all agreed it was a good idea. One day Louis Marion suggested that we visit the snakes that at this time of year gathered in the Coteau near Old Wives Lake.

Every afternoon, thousands of them would lie in the sun in a few large buffalo wallows. The deep depressions contained several big rubbing stones and were surrounded by brush. For a long distance around them the grass was covered with snakes. Every stone twisted as if it were a living thing. As we rode in, a hiss rose from all sides and sent a chill through me.

Our horses were skittish. We hobbled them back from the wallows, and with a few fast steps Louis Marion and I reached the biggest stone. As we jumped to the top snakes rolled off in waves. Every bush and stone was coiled with them. Some had twisted into ropes as thick as the body of a horse. On the sunny side they lay so tightly heaped together that I saw nothing but their heads, all raised to watch me. And they were beautiful. All these brilliant eyes, these tongues flickering, and the unceasing hissing falling on my ears. The westering sun ricocheted rainbow colours from each of their scales. Augustin and Edouard stood on one nearby stone, Isidore and Damase on another, all as transfixed as me.

Then Louis Marion broke the spell. "Serpents," he cried. "This young lunatic plans to marry. Give him your advice."

The answering hiss blocked out every other sound. When it subsided Louis Marion said, "Ha! You heard? Avoid poisonous plants and Blackfoot camps, and guard that beautiful woman from your friends. Good counsel, I would say."

Norbert Welsh was not the only Métis who turned against us. One day a fat braggart named Tom McKay arrived at Batoche with Hillyard Mitchell, who was a good friend to the Métis. Mitchell was trying to arrange a truce between the police and us, so there would not be any fighting. I respected him for that, but McKay swaggered in and demanded that we immediately give ourselves up to the police.

He faced Riel and said, "There seems to be great excitement here, Mr. Riel, and you are the cause of it all. I am commissioned by Major Crozier to insist that you put down your weapons immediately. Your soldiers and officers can remain here, but you and Gabriel Dumont must surrender yourselves as prisoners. For the good of everyone who follows you, give yourselves up. You have deceived poor Gabriel Dumont. He is terribly confused. He doesn't understand what is happening."

Riel said, "No, there is no excitement here; the Métis people simply want redress for their grievances. Many times they asked for their rights and have waited fifteen long years for an answer. Now, after waiting so patiently, their rights will be granted."

McKay opened his mouth, but before he could speak, I said, "Tom, you are the mistaken one. I am no child. I have not been roped and led by the neck. When someone explains something to me, I understand it. I have been struggling for years to get redress for our grievances—since the St. Laurent commune and before. Where have *you* been for all that time? I work *for* my people, not against them—I would never act on behalf of our enemies. I am not like you. Because you are a Métis, you will benefit from any rights we gain. Whatever happens, you have made certain that you won't lose. Have your brains turned to wood? You are a spy and an imbecile. You have no true Métis blood in you. You don't even have a spoonful of good sense in you. You are too stupid even to shut up and listen when you are in an enemy camp. If I didn't respect Hillyard Mitchell and the flag of truce he is under, I would imprison you right now. So heed what I say. Shut up, fool, and do not make me angrier than you have already made me."

Riel accused McKay of having ignored the Métis. He said that McKay was a traitor to his blood and to his Government; that he was a speculator and a scoundrel, a thief and a criminal. Then we played him a joke. I sat down on a keg of syrup and with me as judge and Riel prosecuting we put him on trial for his life. We listed his violations against his Métis blood and asked for his defense. He panicked and shouted that all we wanted was blood and flailed his arms about as he defended himself, knocking over a small cup of blood soup that had been brought for Riel's lunch.

There were some other dishes on the table. Riel raised his soup spoon and said, "So now I won't have any blood, either? You are a Scot, a traitor to your people, and all the blood I had here is spilled. Maybe you should replace it?" Riel put the spoon up to McKay's face and pointed to it. McKay was terrified and said, "If you think you will benefit your cause by taking my blood, you are welcome to it."

This was too much for Riel. He shouted that McKay was a liar and a fool for claiming that the whole country had risen against us. Then he took Mitchell upstairs to speak privately with him while I kept McKay below with me.

As McKay and Mitchell left McKay said, "You French Métis speak so bravely, but I will return and we will see who the real men are."

THOMAS MCKAY, *traitor against the Métis cause*

Riel accused me of neglecting the Métis. I told him that if he took as deep an interest in them as he professed to, then he had neglected them a very long time himself. He said there were two curses in the country—the Government and the Hudson's Bay Company—and that I was a traitor to the Métis cause, a speculator, a scoundrel, and a robber, and I don't know what all else.

There were some little dishes on the table, and he took hold of a spoon and said, "You have no blood. You are a traitor to your people. Your blood is frozen, and all the little blood you have will be in this spoon in five minutes." Then he called his committee together and tried to put me on trial for my life. Gabriel Dumont took a seat and acted as the judge.

Despite Hillyard Mitchell's brave attempt, we had no intention of negotiating with Crozier. Nevertheless, Riel sent two delegates with Mitchell to meet Crozier halfway. Charles Nolin and Maxime Lépine carried a note from Riel informing Crozier that if the police surrendered their weapons to us, we would permit them all to leave on their word of honour that they would not disturb the peace. But Mitchell and McKay were the nose, and I knew that the rest of the body would soon follow behind.

21 March 1885

Major Crozier:

The Councillors of the Provisional Government of the Saskatchewan have the honour to communicate to you the following conditions of surrender: you will be required to give up completely the situation which the Canadian Government has placed you in at Carlton and Battleford, together with all Government properties.

In case of acceptance, you and your men will be set free on your word of honour to keep the peace. And those who choose to leave the country will be furnished with teams and provisions to reach Qu'Appelle.

In case of non-acceptance, we intend to attack you tomorrow, when the Lord's day is over, and to commence without delay a war of extermination upon those who have shown themselves hostile to our rights.

The Exovedate of the Saskatchewan

Of course, the police did not lay down their weapons. On the 25th of March they began to show themselves on the riverbank opposite Batoche.

I said to Riel, "You are giving our enemies all the advantages. We said we would stand up against them, but we sit here at Batoche while they move freely across our country. If we move now, we can catch them by surprise. I know that they will go to Duck Lake. We could catch them crossing the lake and capture the supplies and weapons in Hillyard Mitchell's store at the same time."

Riel said, "It won't be easy."

"Give me some men and leave it to me," I said.

I picked from the most reliable men: my brother Edouard, Philippe Gariépuy, Baptiste Deschamps, Baptiste Arcand, Baptiste Ouellette, Norbert Delorme, Joseph Delorme, and my cousin Augustin. Above of all, Riel insisted that we not fire the first shot.

We left Batoche an hour after noon. Mitchell knew that we were coming and had locked his store. An English-speaking Métis named Magnus Burnstein, who was a farmer at Duck Lake, lived nearby and was a clerk in the store. He told me it was locked.

"Fine," I said. "We will batter down the door."

As I moved toward it Burnstein said, "Hold on. They left me the keys. Here. Take them."

All the guns were gone, but we found some lead shot in the latrine ditch. A little while later Riel arrived from Batoche with all our soldiers. When he arrived, I decided to take my ten men to scout the Carlton trail. I suspected that the police would try a surprise attack. We crossed Duck Lake on the ice and stopped to rest our horses at the reserve. At twilight I sent Baptiste Arcand and Baptiste Ouellette to watch the road. Before long they returned to tell me that there were two police agents on the prowl.

With my brother Edouard, Baptiste Deschamps, Philippe Gariépuy, and an Indian who wanted to accompany us, I rode out to capture the two policemen. "If they try to defend themselves," I said, "we kill them. Otherwise don't hurt them." We left at a gallop by the light of the moon.

We spoke in whispers as we returned to the exact spot where Arcand and Ouellette had first seen the police. On the bluff at the edge of the woods we saw two men riding side by side. We rode toward them under cover, and when we reached the top of the bluff we were near enough to charge. "Go!" I shouted, "Let your horses loose! Capture them!"

There was a thick crust on the snow, so it was impossible to leave the path. I had the best horse but waited for the others to reach the top of the hill before I let him run. When everyone reached the top we were right behind them, as I had hoped. I rode hard on the left side of the two men and called, "Stop! If you try to escape I will kill you." One of the men was Ross, who was a sheriff at Duck Lake.

"What do you want?" asked the other man. "I am a surveyor."

"Don't take me for an imbecile," I answered. "What could you be surveying out here at this time of night?"

I threw my leg across the neck of my horse and seized Ross by the arms. We tumbled into the snow together. Gariépuy and Deschamps chased the other man, but because of me the road was blocked and they could not catch him. Deschamps screamed out to me, "I will shoot him."

There is no doubt the police agent heard him and understood. He turned to look back, and the movement changed the balance of his horse. It stumbled, and he fell off into the snow. Deschamps was immediately on him and without stopping his horse he jumped down and seized the policeman by the arms. Gariépuy arrived at the same time to help.

When we had disarmed them, I said, "You are my prisoners. I am taking you to Duck Lake." They asked for horses. I chose the worst horses we had with us, ones with no saddles on them. "You can use these," I said, "but we will not give you back your own." They preferred to walk.

We five Métis hunters must have terrified Ross, because later he said there were fifty of us. When we returned to Mitchell's store, one of our other prisoners demanded to see sheriff Ross. "He is not sheriff this evening," I laughed. "Tonight he is my guest, just like you."

We went back to the same spot to watch the Carlton trail, but saw nothing more that night. Darkness bled itself into day. After daybreak we thought the police would not risk another attempt on us. We had just stabled our horses when someone cried: "Here come the police!"

In fact it was three more police scouts. Quickly we chose our horses. Some of my men had already left by the time I got my horse saddled. I wanted to be first so instead of staying on the path I tried to cross the snow. I had confidence in my horse, but he got caught in a deep drift and I lost more time. I was a quarter of a mile behind Patrice Fleury and Jim Short, who is my brother-in-law, when the police scouts were joined by Tom McKay. McKay shouted: "Quickly! Save yourselves, or Gabriel will take you prisoner, just like the others."

By then, my brother Edouard had joined Fleury and Short and the three of them chased the three scouts nearly back to the main troop of policemen. Suddenly they found themselves facing twenty sleighs. One was turned sideways, and as they approached it a policeman shouted, "Stop or we will kill you!"

They stopped but stayed on their horses. When I saw them sitting in plain view I screamed, "Get off your horses. Prepare to defend yourselves."

I slipped quickly to the earth and chased my horse away with a slap on the neck. Then I took le Petit and advanced toward the police. When I was about twenty-five yards away, a sergeant called, "If you don't stop, I will kill you!"

Then he saw le Petit. My blood was up. I cocked my gun, aimed it at him, and screamed, "Now you die." He quietly put his rifle across his lap. In two or three jumps I was on him. He had no time to raise his rifle before I hit him on the chest with the barrel of le Petit. He fell back into the sleigh, and my rifle, which was pointed up in the air, accidentally went off. The sergeant struggled to get back up.

"Don't even move, or I will kill you," I told him.

Tom McKay, who was on horseback a short distance away, called, "Take care Gabriel. If you don't stop, this will be the end of you."

I grew furious and shouted, "Someone told me that men were coming against me, but all I see is you, you imbecile. I never would have believed it, but you really are an enemy scout. You are the one who had better watch out, McKay. I will blow out your brains. This is all your fault, all of it. You brought the police here, and everything that is happening right now is your responsibility. Beware of the real Métis warriors I have fighting here with me, traitor."

McKay tried to retort to me, to rear his horse over me, but I swung my rifle at him. He fought to turn his horse, but its back legs slipped off the trail and sank deep in the snow. He was now lower than I was, and I had a better chance of hitting him. I swung again, but the horse reared and the end of my rifle glanced off McKay's back. He spurred his horse and it leaped forward. I took another swing, but only struck the horse's ass.

Another policeman took aim at me. But when I turned le Petit on him he put his gun away. At this moment, all the sleighs started moving. Jim Short and Patrice Fleury had remained on horseback at a distance. Only Edouard had advanced with me toward the sleighs. As they began to move, Edouard tried to climb on one of them. He wanted to take the whole convoy prisoner. The men in the sleigh pushed him down and he fell in the snow. Then they drove over him, and all the sleighs left at a gallop toward Carlton.

McKay commanded the retreat, and I called, "What did you come here for, anyway?"

"I wanted to speak with you," he shouted.

"Well speak then, blockhead," I called. "Don't run away. Be the great man you say you are." But I didn't have enough men to chase them.

Edouard was not injured. Jim Short sat on his horse howling abuse at the sleighs. I shouted at him: "You didn't even get off your horse, so don't fire off your mouth. Your feet will stay warm if this is how you plan to fight this war." And from that moment until the end of the rebellion, he fought like a tiger.

Back at Duck Lake, we stabled our horses and sat down to eat. We had just finished our meal when old Assiyiwin entered from Beardy's reserve. "Major Crozier comes with one hundred men," said the old man. "He tried to sneak across our reserve, but we would not let him. Now he sends me ahead to tell you that he wants a conference."

I had confidence in Assiyiwin, who was half blind but had once been a great warrior and never lied. We had only twenty-five men, so we waited for the police on the big hill beside the trail. First a small band of scouts arrived. While we chased them I told my brother, Isidore, "I don't want to kill them. I want to take prisoners. If they try to kill us, *then* we will kill them." Isidore said, "Right now you are too hot-headed to parley with Crozier. Let me do the talking."

I put most of my men in a small depression on the hilltop to watch the trail, but sent a few others to occupy a small cabin with a clear view of the place where the police were stopping. When the police arrived, they pulled their sleighs off the trail. There was no pattern, but they were well placed for defense. Assiyiwin and Isidore walked out carrying a white flag. Not far from the trail, there was a low foundation wall. I left the trail and was soon at the wall. This time all twenty-five of my men jumped off their horses and prepared to defend themselves.

Crozier himself came forward with Joe McKay as his interpreter—Joe McKay is no relation to Tom McKay. Isidore and McKay were armed. McKay was on horseback. Crozier and Assiyiwin, who were not armed, put their hands out. But McKay moved his horse forward, and Assiyiwin put a hand up to move his rifle away. McKay shook Assiyiwin's hand off and shot Isidore, then turned and shot Assiyiwin. As Crozier ran back toward the sleighs, the police fired a volley at us.

Most people believe that Assiyiwin was the first victim of the war, but Isidore was killed first. Assiyiwin was not armed. My brother had a rifle and Joe McKay had to shoot Isidore so he would not be killed himself. Isidore died because I could not control my temper. He died without firing his gun, which we found by his side. Edouard said that after the first shot he saw Assiyiwin stumbling across the snow. The old warrior did not die quickly, not until after we returned to Duck Lake. Riel baptised him before he died, with Charles Trottier as his godfather.

Against his will Charles Nolin had come with us. And once again his fear overpowered him. At the first shot, he fled in panic to Prince Albert, where he turned himself in. He had discussed our plans with the priests, and his wife and family were staying with Father Vegreville, so although he had not yet betrayed us to the enemy, I believed that he soon would. He suspected that I had decided to execute him. As one of the Métis chiefs, he had betrayed its nation. It was all very tragic. Terror simply overwhelmed him.

After the shooting started we fired as quickly as we could. I shot le Petit a dozen times and was reloading when the English grew alarmed at the number of their dead and began to withdraw. It was time, too, because their cannon was blocked and my soldiers began to surround them. This first engagement lasted half an hour. Riel arrived late and spent most of the fight in the small depression on the top of the hill. He remained on his horse, holding a crucifix in the air. He would not get down and was very exposed. The depression was not deep enough to cover a man on horseback. It was a miracle he was not killed.

As we turned the enemy, I lay hidden behind a small bluff. Across an opening in the trees I saw a sleigh. I shouted to my men, "Courage! Let's make these redcoats jump. I am going to take those sleighs." A policeman showed his face and my bullet to his head knocked him back in the sleigh. Then I laughed, not because I liked killing but to encourage my men.

I was so determined to attack that I didn't think to keep myself under cover. As I closed in on the sleighs, I slipped and fell on the snow. At that very moment a bullet plowed a furrow across the crown of my head, and the ricochet hissed away. I wanted to get up, but the blow had been so violent I couldn't.

Blood gushed up in the air. Joseph Delorme cried out, "Oh no! They have killed Gabriel!"

"Courage Joseph," I called. "They will have to actually take my head before I'll die. The English bullet only grazed me."

Before this fight Delorme had said, "I was never under fire, and I am afraid. Keep me charged up." All during the battle at Duck Lake, he fought like a lion at my side, and he really was extraordinarily courageous. During the last battle at Batoche a bullet went though his thigh and tore off both his testicles. When the English found him there were big flaps of skin on either side of his wound. They wanted to put him to sleep as they closed the wound, but he refused their drugs. To show them that he was unafraid he laughed as they operated.

After reassuring Joseph Delorme, I called to Baptiste Vandal, "Cousin, take my rifle." Vandal dropped his old rifle and took le Petit from me. "Good," I said. "Take my cartridge belt, too." He unhooked the cartridge belt for my revolver. "No! Not that one," I said. "Take the other." Then I tried to struggle to my knees, but my revolver belt had held up my trousers and Baptiste Vandal had not done it back up. So it is true, as the English say, that I was caught with my pants down.

My brother Edouard had been hit over by the side of a small ravine; he slipped and pulled himself to me. I waved him away, telling him to rally our men, and soon he had them shouting in triumph. Only then did my cousin Augustin fall. A bullet hit his arm and tore through his body. A few moments earlier I had told him not to expose himself so much. I dragged myself to him and tried to get to my knees to make the sign of the cross, but fell again on my side. My right side was paralyzed. I whispered, "Do not be afraid Augustin. Soon you will be well." But he had already died. The bullet had passed through his chest. I lay laughing on my side. Through my tears I said, "I am sorry cousin, I owe you a prayer."

Augustin, do you remember?
They will fly over us forever.

By then the English were retreating. Edouard shouted, "After them! Exterminate them all!" But Riel cried, "There has been enough blood spilled! In God's name let them go. We have had enough murder. Let them go."

After the fight they bound my wound with handkerchiefs and put me on my horse. My head was pounding. As we rode back to the village we passed Augustin, then Isidore—all the life had flowed out of him. I got off my horse, but could not tell if he was dead. He was a dark shadow in a spreading red stain on the snow.

A police captain called Morton had hidden behind a tree and killed two of our men. A bullet broke his spine when he tried to flee, and he lay screaming and suffering horribly. Guillaume McKay did him a service by shooting him in the head. They put me back on my horse and tried to tie me there, but I fought them off. A little farther on someone said, "Behind that bluff there is a young volunteer, injured in the leg." I rode around to find him. "Don't worry, my boy," I said. "Be a good little chicken and hold still. This will be quick and painless." He was very young and began to cry. I reached for my revolver, but it was right in the middle of my back and I could not reach it from the left or the right. As I struggled for my gun, Riel arrived and stopped me from killing the wounded volunteer.

ALEXI DUMONT, *adopted son*

You be scared like I was scared that day at Duck Lake, you would never forget either.

I'm shivering—it's cold and we wait for hours on a snow-covered hilltop. No sun. Dull clouds overhead, endless and grey. No horizon, just grey light, snow and the sky a flat screen.

I've sneaked along without a rifle. Gabriel curses because we are too few and Riel is not there with reinforcements and our scouts say that the police have about one hundred men. "*Mahti Pahakitoon*—Shut up! Nobody move!" he shouts, forcing us deeper into the snow; flat and far apart behind our clumps of brush.

The enemy comes—silent little silhouettes on the grey snow. They seem to ride slowly through the sky toward us, floating past the dark leafless trees. As hard and cold as Fate or the will of God.

No gun, so I'm supposed to run down and snatch ammunition and weapons from our dying enemies when we drive them back.

"Even if they don't fall back: any boy who can't outrun a bullet is no bloody good," says Gabriel with a smile.

"*Prenez garde!*"

Gabriel's eldest brother, my uncle Isidore, strides across the field, carrying a white flag. Two men move out to meet him. A shot. Another. Ducking my head as the first volley patters into the hillside—far too low. I'm a better marksman than these redcoats and volunteers. Too bad I don't have a gun.

Before they came Jerome Delorme roared: "Those policemen shoot badly; the volunteers are no good at all." We all cheered, but Gabriel said, "Men can very quickly learn to shoot well."

Once I asked him what it's like to kill a man. "Not much different from killing game," he said, "only in a fight the game is shooting back."

Two dull thumps. Gabriel flings himself down near me, worms to the crest of the hill, and fires le Petit at the cannon crew—cursing them viciously. The big gun stops. He leaps back on his horse, rushing off somewhere else.

Riel has arrived. Refuses to get down off his horse; sits in plain sight just behind the battle line, bullets buzzing around him. Waves a huge crucifix, calling on our God to give us victory, to drive off the invaders.

Gabriel has fallen. I see the blood spattered around him and watch him staunch his head wound with hands full of snow. I see him crawl to his dying cousin Augustin Laframboise and try to make the sign of the cross over him. I see him fall shaking onto his side. My uncle Isidore lies stretched out still.

Our enemies mill around their sleighs. A wounded volunteer, unable to rise on damaged legs, struggles toward his friends. One boot scuffles, a little push and he writhes a few inches forward. Snow curls aside from his head like sod from a plow. A blood line marks his trail. I watch him for a long time, while the teams are hitched and the wounded loaded onto the sleighs. I want to call out to the police to wait. They don't. The wounded man is still plowing blindly toward the empty road.

Then we are cheering and I'm on my feet, joining our warriors stripping guns and cartridge belts from the dying and the dead. Gabriel's brother Edouard is screaming for us to chase the enemy, and Riel is shouting for us not to.

PHILIPPE GARNOT, *Secretary to the Exovedate*

All is confusion. A woman wearing a red petticoat has a knife in her hand and is ready for butchery. "I want to eat two of these prisoners," she screams. We hold her back. An injured man arrives. He shouts in a loud voice that he wants a prisoner so he can dine. We hold him back too.

Next Gabriel Dumont arrives, his face all bloody. He has handkerchiefs bound around his head and seems drunk. We help him down from his horse and ask if he wants his wounds dressed. No, first he wants the prisoners. "Out! It's time to die!" he shouts, bursting in on them. With blows he drives them outside, where they stand blinking stupidly in the light. He raises his rifle, then stops abruptly, the colour draining from his face. His head sinks tiredly down. My men lead him away to dress his wounds. I take the prisoners back inside.

A wagon carries in another prisoner, this one with a leg wound. I don't recognize him, but he calls me by name. I take pity on him, help him up to the room where we keep the others.

Finally the bodies of our dead arrive. It is so sad; they look so pathetic. One hour earlier Jose and Baptiste Montour, Captain Isidore Dumont, and Captain Auguste Laframboise had been strong men. Now their corpses lie pale and yellow. Twenty-six combatants on our side—four dead and two wounded. During the night the old Indian Assiyiwin dies. He does not die easily.

Had we followed Gabriel Dumont's wishes, things might have turned out better. There certainly would not have been so many witnesses for the Crown.

ALEX STEWART, *prisoner*

From the sounds of the gunfire, I would say that the fight at Duck Lake lasted about half an hour. Then the Indians came howling back, saying in Cree, "We have killed nine volunteers and three policemen." Old Gabriel Dumont, who got a bullet wound in the head in the first action and was unconscious during the fight, rode up and said, "Bring out the prisoners so I can have my revenge." The Indians took up his yell and things looked very black for us. Riel, however, rode up, and after some talking and the intervention of some sensible men, saved us.

You ask why I wanted to kill wounded men and prisoners? They came as aggressors with cannons to fight against us. We didn't start the fight and Isidore was murdered under a flag of truce. They murdered my brother and my favourite cousin, and wounded Edouard and me. I was not thinking clearly, but they were cowards who left nine corpses and one wounded man on the field of battle. When they fled, they made sure to take policemen, but left the dead volunteers behind. We lost five good men, including Assiyiwin, who came to us on their behalf.

After the battle, Riel collected the fighters and said, "Today the world rained blood, but we prevailed. Thank God who gave you such a valiant chief. Give three cheers! Hooray for Gabriel Dumont."

I waited until they finished, then let them help me off my horse and bandage my head. The bullet had plowed a furrow two inches long and three quarters of an inch deep across the top of my skull. Fortunately I have a thick skull, or I would certainly have been killed. For two full days afterward I was too stunned to think. Every time I coughed it was like a hammer striking me on the head, and several times I lost consciousness. One time I blacked out, fell on my face on a heap of iron at a blacksmith's shop. This scarred me, so I am not as pretty as I once was.

The priest says, "There has been a miracle here."
Where? What is so different here? Isidore and Augustin have not been
resurrected. My wound has not healed itself.

The weather remained frosty and our dead enemies lay exposed. The sun came out the day after we buried our own dead, so I insisted that we send some men out to put the enemy corpses in the cabin near the battlefield. The dead volunteers had probably not borne any hatred against us, and their bodies were already beginning to swell. It was terrible to leave them outdoors to rot and for the coyotes and birds to feast on. I also suggested that we send a prisoner to Carlton to tell the English to come and take their dead. Riel thought they would be afraid to come, so in a letter to the police I gave my word of honour that none of my men would disturb them. Riel and I signed the safe conduct and sent the prisoner off with it, but the police arrested him as a spy. Panic took hold of them, and they abandoned Fort Carlton during the night, setting fire to it as they fled. Happily, my scouts put the fire out and saved most of the supplies the police had left behind.

Duck Lake, March 27th 1885

To Major Crozier
Commanding Officer
Fort Carlton.

Sir,

A Calamity fell upon the country yesterday. You are responsible for it before God and men.

Your men cannot claim that their intentions were peaceable, since they were bringing along cannons. And they fired many shots first.

God has been pleased to grant us the victory: and as our movement is to save our rights, our victory is good: and we offer it to the Almighty.

Major, we are Christians in war as in peace. We write you in the name of God and of humanity to come and take away your dead whom we respect. Come and take them tomorrow before noon.

LOUIS "DAVID" RIEL,
Exovede
PIERRE PARENTEAU
ALBERT MONKMAN
DONALD ROSS

J-BTE BOUCHER

AMB. JOBIN

GABRIEL DUMONT

MOÏSE OUELLETTE

DAMASE CARRIÈRE

DAVID TOUROND

NORBERT DELORME

MAXIME LÉPINE

BTE. PARENTEAU

PH. GARNOT, *Secretary*

PIERRE GARIÉPUY

The men I sent to move the bodies of our enemies returned laughing. Lawrence Clarke had joined the police for their attack, and in his hurry to flee he threw off his thick winter coat and a cap of wild cat fur. They showed the coat and cap to us; we all recognized them.

I wanted to ambush the police as they fled from Fort Carlton. They had to pass through a spruce forest, where we could easily attack them. Saint Denis, one of the Métis at Carlton who had put out the fire, wrote, "If you would come with me to the black spruces we can destroy them all." When Riel opposed me I was upset. "If you continue to give them these advantages," I said, "we cannot win."

The police took three days before they began to believe our prisoner's story. How surprised they were to read the letter from Riel and me. They were free to recover their dead, and we even offered some help. Three English Métis from Prince Albert came to do the job, and several of my men helped them. We also released the prisoner with the wounded leg to them.

One or two days after the English came for their dead we left Duck Lake. We burned all the buildings there but the mill. Then we remained at Batoche and did nothing for nearly one month. Some papers we found at Carlton told us that the Canadian Government was sending its army against us. Friends at Qu'Appelle and other places sent us constant messages. Poundmaker sent four messengers with letters and the news. A bunch of newspapers came to us from Qu'Appelle that described the movements of Middleton's army, and we captured a man named McConnell who carried a letter in code with him. We could not understand it, but we tricked him into telling us that Middleton had reached Clarke's Crossing with seven hundred men, and that the letter outlined the times for simultaneous attacks that they had planned.

I kept my scouts constantly on the move. I wanted a corps of them to follow the troops and harass them at night. By preventing the Canadians from sleeping I thought that we could demoralize them. "Three days without sleep, and they will be at each other's throats," I said. But Riel disagreed with me. He said it was too much like the way Indians fought, and that it would upset the friends we had among the troops. I said, "Whoever travels with an English army is no friend to the Métis. I don't have any scruples about harassing them. We are the smaller force. We must do everything we can to reduce the odds against us. I will take some men and blow up the railroad, which is no help to us. It only serves to bring more of them to attack and kill us."

But no matter how strenuously I argued, Riel only said, "If you knew these men as I do, you would not want to treat them this way." So I listened and gave up my plan. Although I was convinced that from a human point of view mine was the best plan, I had absolute confidence in his faith and his prayers, and that God would listen to him.

PHILIPPE GARNOT, *Secretary to the Exovedate*

Whenever Riel heard a Métis warrior swearing, he would immediately say: "Quickly! Beg for God's forgiveness."

One day he said this to Louis Marion, and Marion said, "I would ask His forgiveness, but by God, He never listens to me."

Riel said, "That doesn't matter. You must beg, and not offend Him. He hears everything. He loves you and will answer your prayers. Beg His forgiveness, and mine too."

"Ah well," said Marion with a smile, "I guess I don't try to restrain myself. Damn it all! I beg His pardon, and yours too."

Marion was not the only one who swore; there were some even among the Exovedate, and Riel grew very discouraged with all the blaspheming. Still, he told us absolutely not to trust the priests because they didn't follow God's laws either. He said that the priests only wanted to make money for the Church, and that they had no intention of assisting us unless we permitted them to control every aspect of our lives. "Is it freedom to do only what a priest permits you to do?" Riel asked.

I was relieved when one day two of my scouts entered and told a story that confirmed Riel's confidence in God. Elzéar Parisian and Yellow Blanket had been stalking Middleton's column when they suddenly found themselves face to face with a squad of about thirty policemen. They fled out onto the prairie. Parisian's horse was poor and he had only a shotgun. Yellow Blanket was well mounted and well armed. When the police began to catch them, Yellow Blanket slowed down and fired from the saddle. The English could not fire accurately from the saddle and had to get down to shoot. Nevertheless, they finally got so near that Yellow Blanket, who was a Catholic, said, "Brother, we must pray to the Almighty to take pity on us." They began to pray and immediately reached the security of a wooded place, where they fired from cover and drove off the police.

Riel said that this proved God was with us. He gave Yellow Blanket a horse for his bravery and said, "The Spirit of God came to me and said: 'Not far from here.' So I know that our conflict with the English will be resolved here, at Batoche. There is no point in going out to fight the English. Batoche is where it will all end."

The Exovedate was discussing whether or not we should declare ourselves a sovereign nation and ask for help from the United States. One morning Riel said to me, "Uncle Gabriel, last night I had a dream. The Spirit of God placed me in a cart with Michel Dumas. He left for the United States. I accompanied him part of the way and we spoke about the United States, then I left him. I returned, and he continued. As I watched him leave, I noticed an enormous, snake accompanying him. The snake was alone, but he was huge and menacing and sprouted feathers like leaves that glittered and flashed all the colours and shades of green. I didn't think a lot about it. I turned to go back to Batoche. The region around *me* was clear and open; but all the rest of the plain swarmed with snakes. There were more snakes than I could count. Oh! It is dangerous to ask the Americans for aid."

Finally, on April 22nd, I could wait no longer for the will of God to save us. Riel and I argued. Before the Exovedate he insisted that I not attack the soldiers. "The Spirit Who Guides me said that the battle would not be far from Batoche," he said. "It told me to bind our prisoners, which indicates that we need all our men here at Batoche. It told me to defend every inch of earth, which indicates that we must keep all our strength at Batoche."

I said, "No! I won't give our enemies these advantages. I won't permit them to move unopposed across *my* country. 'Defending every inch of the country' means that we must go out and make them fight their way here. I won't wait like a rabbit frozen by a snake."

He said, "The Spirit Who Guides me says: 'Gabriel Dumont! Pay attention!' Uncle Gabriel, fear your reckless courage and your wild habit of exposing yourself. If anything happens to you, it will not simply be a misfortune for your friends but an irreparable loss for the army and to the nation. Uncle Gabriel, if your injury were healed I would be more disposed to let you harass our enemies. If we had some reinforcements, I could change my opinion."

"Exovede," I said, "the time for waiting is past. Your concern for the well-being of our enemies is remarkable, but they are on us and I won't surrender to them without a fight. This is my country, too. I can not accept your humanitarian concerns. Their general shows his weakness by hesitating, despite the fact that his army outnumbers ours. I will go and attack him—with the army if it will follow me, but alone if I must. If we don't hit them now, then the weak and hesitant among us will become even more afraid when they hear the weeping of their women and children at their backs."

The council agreed with my plan. We would lay a trap for the soldiers near Touronds' Coulee. Riel said, "It is in God's hands. Do as you wish."

All rebellions dissolve in wind, but what of that—the wind is wiser than we. It embraces its time and season. It blusters and changes, spins and whirls across the open spaces, through the trees, over rivers and lakes. Whatever course it chooses, it follows with abandon. When the wind grows calm, it is awaiting its next opportunity.

Despite Riel's conviction that God was with us, throughout the time that he insisted we remain at Batoche I had not remained idle. I had scouts following every column— my man Jerome Henry was a teamster with Middleton's baggage train. Special messengers went out to every Indian who had ever smoked my tobacco. Isidore Parenteau and Louis Letendre snowshoed to the Assiniboines at Battle River in the Eagle Hills, and Poundmaker told me that his men were sitting on their heels, ready to rise up at the first signal.

I sent François Vermette and Napoléon Carrière to Round Prairie with gifts for the Sioux and the Métis there. They skirted Saskatoon because of the Orangemen. But on their return, Norbert Welsh rode with the Orangemen to stop them from joining us.

"Where are you going?" asked Welsh. "I go back to Batoche to fight," said Charles Trottier. Welsh said, "What business is it of yours?" Trottier and the Sioux answered, "The Batoche Métis are our brothers. We are going to help them, so stand aside." So Welsh stood back, which was wise because he faced sixty Sioux and a dozen well-armed Métis, all of them very resolute.

Some miles north of Round Prairie, those reinforcements saw an old Irishman and his wife and children scrambling over the snow. Trottier sent his son after them. He caught them standing with their naked feet on a blanket. When Trottier finally got the family warmed up, the Irishman confessed that he had mistaken our men for the Orangemen, who had been threatening him because he was a Catholic.

My emissaries to the Assiniboines didn't have such good luck. They could not recruit reinforcements for us, but brought back news that Poundmaker had organized an attack on Fort Pitt. The Métis at Horse Butte had agreed to help him. They sent some messengers to ask us what our plans were. Poundmaker's diversion was welcome. I sent ten men to urge the Horse Butte Métis to hurry and join with Poundmaker and attack the fort. That was when I also tried to send a message to Big Bear.

Edouard rode to Fort à la Corne to bring our brother Elie and some other Métis back to fight with us. When my brothers reached Batoche they had a herd of Government cattle with them. "Look what the Government gave us," shouted Elie. "Let's eat."

Anonymous report to the Toronto Mail:

As we marched north we encountered the first Métis homes that many of us had ever seen. They were all open, and the interiors showed evident signs of comfort and prosperity. In every other house a fiddle hung on the wall, to help in whiling away the long winter evenings. The sight bred among many of us a feeling that these half breeds are being wronged. These were the houses of men who had too much to lose to embark lightly on rebellion.

The sight of these comfortable homes, coupled with the knowledge that the men who raised them, after suffering the rigours of frontier life and fostering a love for the very soil itself, can not raise $10 as mortgage to title on one thousand acres, brings home to everyone the reality of their residents' grievance.

Middleton may really have had a bullet pierce his fur cap at Fish Creek, as he reported. It may even have been one of my bullets. But he can congratulate himself that I didn't recognize him. If I had, he would be dead.

At twilight the day after the Exovedate accepted my plan, I collected one hundred and fifty fighters and began to march south. Ammunition was so scarce that each fighter had only twenty cartridges. My brother Edouard remained behind to guard Batoche, but Riel rode with us. Every few miles he insisted that we stop and say a rosary. At Roger Goulet's farm we killed two cows to eat. We had just finished our meal when two messengers arrived from Edouard bringing news that a troop of police had been seen on the Qu'Appelle road riding toward Batoche. Edouard wanted Riel or me to return with men enough to strengthen the defense forces.

I didn't believe the story and refused to turn back. "I left planning to attack Middleton, and I won't return to Batoche until I fight him," I said. Riel agreed to return, so I took this opportunity to eliminate the most faint-hearted men from my troop.

When Riel and his fifty chosen men rode away, another small prayer leaped unbidden to my lips: "Thank you, Lord, for permitting me to move more quickly."

With one hundred committed warriors I rode on. Had we found Middleton's camp this night his soldiers would have been very lucky to survive. They were completely unprepared for us. Jerome Henry had convinced Middleton that we were too superstitious to attack at night. I planned on attacking his camp in the dark, setting the grass on fire and taking advantage of the confusion to massacre all of them. However, it was very foggy and nearly daylight when we finally reached McIntosh's farm, where Middleton was camped.

Within a very short time they seemed to have discovered us, so just before daybreak I led my men back to Fish Creek, where we could ambush the soldiers as they crossed Touronds' Coulee. We camped at the Touronds' farm—it seemed years since we had all gathered to meet Riel those few hopeful months before. I gave orders not to leave any tracks near the trail, but my young men had never been on a buffalo hunt and did not understand discipline. Some of them camped right on the trail. They were playing as if war was a game, and some of them rode out to hunt the livestock.

I didn't realize what was happening because Napoléon Nault and I had gone ahead to scout the enemy position. We had decided to hunt the police scouts the way wolves hunt little dogs. I let Napoléon watch the trail and went half a mile farther on. From a high point, I saw some enemy scouts pursue a group of my men. I tried to draw the enemy down into the woods behind me where Napoléon could come on them from the side. I heard their bugle signals, but they would not follow me.

Finally Napoléon Nault and I returned to our camp. At about seven o'clock, Gilbert Breland reported that a column of eight hundred soldiers was advancing toward us. I placed most of my men in a cavity in the bank of the coulee facing the Touronds' house. Then I took twenty men ahead to where we could attack the soldiers on the flank when the main body of my force turned them. We remained on horseback. Everyone had strict orders not to attack until the whole enemy column had moved into the coulee.

Unfortunately, the English Métis who scouted for our enemies saw the signs my young men had left. They stopped Middleton, who sent more scouts ahead to examine the coulee. One of the English scouts worked his way slowly toward my position. I held my fire, not wanting to waste a cartridge or reveal my presence. "Let them all come," I told my men. "When they get near enough, we will take them and their weapons."

The primary thought in my mind was that we must capture more guns and ammunition. When the scout saw us and fled, I chased after him, hoping to knock him out of the saddle and get his gun before he could warn the others. I was so intent on him that some of my men had to shout to warn me that about forty policemen had reached the edge of the coulee. To my regret, I could not capture that policeman's weapon. When I realized that I would not catch him before he reached his friends, I shot him and drove my horse over into the thick brush in the coulee.

As I worked my way towards Middleton, some of his troops began to fire. Several of my men had rejoined our main unit, but I got off my horse and slipped nearer to the enemy. In the bottom of the coulee I found a young Cree, and together we moved from bluff to bluff to scout the enemy. It was not long before we found them: they were very near. I decided to draw their fire. We fired our rifles and flattened ourselves to the earth. They could not tell where the shots had come from, so we fired again. When the enemy located the smoke of our guns, they fired into the grove where we lay sheltered. I don't know how many of them I hit because I took cover after every shot, but I could not have missed very often. Finally, the branches breaking around us forced us to withdraw.

It began to rain. I met a bunch of Sioux warriors, who told me that one of their companions had been killed on the slope above us. I climbed up to retrieve his weapons, but someone had already taken them. He had not died, but was only wounded. And he was singing, trying to encourage the rest of us. I asked if his wounds were mortal, he said no. Bullets hissed thick and fast around me as I crawled back across the mud to rally my fighters.

Napoléon Nault was one of the few courageous men who stayed with me in the coulee. "We must rejoin the main unit," he called. We jumped on our horses and raced back. Of one hundred and thirty men that I had placed in the cavity, only forty-seven remained. Of my twenty riders I counted only fifteen. Young Ladouceur didn't have a gun; instead he carried a flag of the Virgin.

By now my young men had realized that war is not a game. They had learned to be afraid. "Do not fear the bullets," I called, showing myself to the enemy. "Bullets won't wound you. God takes your head when He wants you, but until then you are in no danger." I showed them how to shoot to hit their marks, and they began to shout with joy.

My head wound had reopened. Every quick movement sent a wave of pain through me. Every cannon shot was a blow to my skull. Blood filled my hat. Bursts of white light dazzled me, but I could not pause. The young men gave me their guns to shoot whenever le Petit was empty, and reloaded my rifle for me. By now a small group of us had worked nearer to the enemy. I saw an officer aim at us and shot him. We watched him fall, heard him crying like a child. My young men laughed, asking loudly if he was still enjoying his adventure. I later heard that he died.

The wind blew from behind us toward them. When we had only seven cartridges left, I said, "We will set fire to the grass and advance under cover of the flames and smoke. Shout and sing, and we will force our enemies back." I kept myself in the thickest clouds of smoke, picking my targets carefully. Unfortunately, we didn't capture any weapons or ammunition. Several bodies lay in the open, and there was certainly a dead man in the stream because it ran red with blood; but all the bodies had been stripped of their weapons.

The rain turned to sleet. We were wet and very cold—we had taken off our outer jackets to fight and tied them to our saddles. I led my small troop of seven Métis back toward the forty-seven fighters left in the cavity. They were completely surrounded by the enemy. They fought well, encouraging each other and shouting abuse when the enemy tried to parley. Isidore Dumas began to sing the old Napoleonic song, "Malbrouck." At the chorus my young men joined in: "*Mironton, mironton, mirontaine!*" And for a moment, we drew the fire of the enemy. But we had no more cartridges to fight with, so we retired to the Throunds' farm to eat something.

By twilight, no reinforcements had arrived from Batoche. The forty-seven fought on in the increasing darkness. There was nothing I could do for them and my head was pounding, so I started back toward Batoche where at least there was more ammunition. On the trail I met my brother Edouard, with Baptiste Boucher and eighty riders.

Edouard raged and caught us all up in his fury. He had a wagon for the injured and a buckboard filled with ammunition. When we reached the Touronds', he drove his horse to the edge of the coulee and down into the thick of the battle. The others followed him, shouting and firing their guns as they went. In an instant the English fled like rabbits. They dove into clumps of brush and trees and disappeared, leaving all their baggage behind. There was a cannon there, and thirty-two carbines. The doctor had abandoned his bag and medicines, so we drank to his health from the two gallons of brandy he left behind.

CHARLES TROTTIER, *Métis soldier*

I was at Fish Creek with Gabriel. I descended into the coulee, making a sign to our men with my hand and shouting, "Go for the coulee." We all took off our outer coats and tied our horses and climbed back up the hill on foot to fire. We fired I don't know how many shots. Suddenly I saw a Sioux killed near me. My gun was not good, so I called out to another Sioux to bring me the gun of the dead man. It was a double-barrel gun, with a powder horn and sack of shot. We fired again, and then I saw Gabriel come toward me. He said he didn't have any cartridges; I gave him two as I wanted to use the double-barrel gun. I called out to our fighters, "They want to take the coulee; we must get our horses and stop them." I told one young man to take Gabriel's horse, and I took mine. On the way down I met Gabriel, who asked me where his horse was. I told him that the young man had it. It is the last I saw of Gabriel.

From Batoche I heard the cannons firing, so with three others I headed off for the battlefield. We met two Indians who came too, and then, in the afternoon, we met Gabriel and four or five others riding back from Fish Creek. They were dirty and tired. Gabriel's head wound was open, with blood streaming down his face from under his hat. He was demoralized and didn't want us to carry on. "There are not enough of us," he said. "It is in God's hands. Nothing can be done. Come back to Batoche with me."

But then a group of sixty horsemen rode up to join us. Again Gabriel said it was too late, that the cause was hopeless and we should rest first.

Finally Yellow Blanket leaned close and said to him, "Uncle Gabriel, when your friends need help, you don't wait for the next day."

"Yes," I said, "we must deliver them from their enemies." So Gabriel agreed that we would all go back and he would fight some more.

That is the way it was. Edouard and his eighty riders had saved the day, and I rode back to Tourands' with them. Thanks to Divine Providence, during this whole day of desperate and continuous fighting we had lost just four men—two Sioux warriors, José Vermette, and my nephew Saint-Pierre Parenteau. Two others were injured: my nephew François Boyer, and Cardinal, who died three days later. These are the losses we suffered—the "considerable number" that Middleton claimed we lost.

Middleton is also mistaken when he speaks about our *rifle pits*. Those were nothing more than dips in the trail worn out by walking animals. And the only supplies I left for his soldiers were the remains of the bull we ate at Calixte Tourond's and some chickens in Isaac Tourond's henhouse. Middleton could not have seen the things he talks about in his report, and his scouts misled him. It was easier for him to believe exaggerations than that he was defeated by a handful of badly armed men. Of the one hundred and fifty men who followed me from Batoche, only fifty-four remained on the battlefield at the end of the fight, when my brother Edouard and his eighty riders came to our aid.

The Dumonts paid in blood. Isidore and Augustin,
François Boyer and Saint-Pierre Parenteau all gone,
and me with a hole in my head.

Edouard's troop had brought a wagon for our dead and wounded. Most of the men started back immediately. I tried to stay behind to help the wounded, but by the time we had reached the Touronds' house I knew I could not make it. My pain and weakness embarrassed me, and I wished to be alone. "I want to accompany you," I said to my nephew Jean Dumont, "but I am too sick. My head wound has opened again. You must take over for me and stay with the wagons. I will get to Batoche on my own."

Some miles down the trail, Jean and his friend André Letendre rode up to me. "Where are you going?" I asked them. "What are you doing? If you won't stay with the wounded, I must go back. I am hurt and good for nothing now, Jean. You must act on my behalf." Jean had never before seen me weak and could not believe that I needed his help.

Napoléon Nault and some others found me on the trail with my horse stopped dead and me slumped over almost unconscious in the saddle. Napoléon tore a strip from his saddle blanket to bandage my head. He remained with me until we reached Batoche. It was just getting light when we got there. I needed sleep, but Riel wanted my report. When I had finished, I still could not sleep because some of the more demoralized men were talking about deserting, and I had to stay with them to keep up their courage.

Throughout our battle at Fish Creek, the people at Batoche told me, Riel had remained on his knees praying, his arms stretched out from his sides. When he grew tired, assistants had helped him hold his arms up. He persuaded the women and children to join him, saying that their prayers would protect us. And they did sustain us until Edouard arrived. I credit our victory to Riel.

About that time Riel said, "I dreamed there is a traitor among us. He is a short man and has asked some of the men guarding the other riverbank to desert with him. I know for an absolute fact that two of your men have been asked to betray us."

I remembered that the day we went to scout Duck Lake, Albert Monkman had abandoned his post. He was a short man. He could be the traitor. Patrice Fleury and Garçon Bélanger said that Monkman had asked them to desert with him and before the Exovedate I challenged Monkman to answer to the charges. "Patrice and Garçon have not lied," he said, "but I did not intend to desert. It has come to the final battle, and I have to know for sure whether Riel has second sight."

"So now you know. This is no time for jokes," I told him. "You were once completely one of us, but in your heart you have deserted." When we captured Ross at Duck Lake, I had given his revolver to Monkman. Now I took it back. I had him chained.

I remember he said, "Gabriel. You are being unjust to me," as Patrice led him away.

PHILIPPE GARNOT, *Secretary to the Exovedate*

Monkman had said only two words and made a joke about Riel being a Fenian, not Reilly a Frenchman at all. He was chained and would have been executed if Riel had dared; but by then he began to be afraid of the Council, which had begun to half know him. A proposition like that would completely have unmasked him. As he himself said, only in Gabriel Dumont could he have complete confidence. He had dazzled Gabriel with flatteries and promises.

LOUIS "DAVID" RIEL, *prophet*

Today I saw Gabriel Dumont. He seemed weakened and ashamed. He could not look at me; he only looked down at his bare table. But Gabriel Dumont is blessed. His faith has not faltered. He is strong by the grace of God; his hope and his confidence in God will be justified. He will emerge from this struggle with his table piled high with the spoils of his enemies. Jesus Christ and the Virgin Mary will give him back his joy.

Madeleine and I lost almost every possession we had. After the battle of Fish Creek, the English marched to my farm. They took their vengeance by destroying the precious world we had created, smashing whatever they didn't want or could not carry. They stole the things we valued: Madeleine's books and sewing machine, my billiard table. They burned our house and dismantled the stables, tore apart the store and fences to use as barricades on the *Northcote*. Middleton himself took a packet of my fine furs, perhaps as compensation for the cap he claims I ruined at Fish Creek. There was nothing except Madeleine left for me to protect.

When our wounded men reached Batoche, Madeleine and Old Batoche took care of them, helped by the English prisoners. But the English were not reliable. After Cardinal went mad and died, Madeleine discovered that he had fallen out of bed. She found a bloody piece of his broken skull hidden under his mattress. There were tears in her eyes when she showed it to me. Another time, Anthony Vandal seized my sleeve as I walked by him. He crawled across the floor after me, begging: "Cousin, don't let these Englishmen kill me; don't permit me to die." I gave the piece of Cardinal's skull to Riel and said, "This is too much. We can no longer entrust our wounded to these friendly Englishmen. Even as hostages, their lives are worth nothing. Unless you continue to insist on protecting them, I am going to have them executed here and now."

E.R. JOHNSTON, *reporter to the* St. Paul Pioneer-Press,
May 13 & 16, 1885:

Gabriel Dumont's house was reached about noon of May
4th. It is a double affair, two comfortable storey-and-a-half
houses connected by a short passage. Marks of the comfort in
which the rebel fighter lived were everywhere visible, though
the valuable household goods had been carried away. The
front of the house was painted blue, but this was the only
mark of bad taste shown. Across the road is the store, and
therein the first object to attract attention was a well-worn
pool table. As to merchandise, there was not much to boast of
and the principal objects for looting were boxes of blacking.
Here as elsewhere the observers were impressed with the
substantial comfort of the habitations of these mixed bloods.
Their dwellings and their fittings, their stables and their farms
were far better than those of their cousins in the Red River
valley ten years ago. Among the articles taken away from
Dumont's were a couple of violins, a concertina, and a well-
thumbed copy of the complete works of Shakespeare marked
"Thomas Young, St. Peters, 1862." Norbert Welsh, a scout we
had with us, said that he thought the book was a wedding
present that had been given to Dumont's wife.

We attack tomorrow. We left Fish Creek yesterday morning,
the steamer accompanying us. The steamer reached the
landing opposite Gabriel Dumont's store at three p.m., the
troops camping half a mile from the river bank soon after
noon (on May 7th). The camp was not a desirable one, being
surrounded by bushes and rather inclined to hollowness in the
center. We knew the enemy were not far off, as shots were
fired at some of our party from the west side of the river, and a
rebel picket of six was dislodged by our advance. All guards
were doubled, the men ordered to sleep in their clothes.

By seven a.m. on May 8th, we were en route again. As our column debouched into the open the observant saw, to our rear and riverward, a black column of smoke ascending rapidly. Some of us were posted and knew that Gabriel Dumont's house, store, and barn had been fired. Later we learned by courier that all the buildings and what was left of their contents had been totally destroyed. The pool table was taken to the boat by S.L. Bedson, and will be set up in his home. It was about all that was left to loot. How deeply ingrained in every man is the love of law-breaking! I took the long and difficult walk to Dumont's yesterday after we had camped. Though laden with a Snider rifle and a couple of cartridge pouches, I loaded myself down with the following spoils of war:

—One four-legged stool, which was left when we broke camp this morning.
—Six pepper boxes, which I distributed among as many messes.
—Eight papers of large pins, which may be useful to the medical attendants.
—One large delft platter, 14 x 10 inches, on the edge of which I dropped my gun just after I reached camp. Enough of the dish remained intact to serve as center ornament for the mess table.
—Four penholders. We haven't any pens, and ink is as scarce as diamonds in this camp.
—One tin teaspoon.
—One can of white paint; ditto blue paint; neither of any earthly use.
—Two boxes of hair pins (very useful, of course), and as many of china buttons.

Everybody else looted in similar wholesale fashion, and with about as little discrimination.

We did not have many fighting men at Batoche for the final battle, but every one had some special talent. One Sioux warrior who came with White Cap had lost his wife and family at the Little Big Horn. He hated all white soldiers and was very good with rifles. He kept all the weapons we had in good repair. I don't know what became of him after the battle, but without him we would have had even fewer guns than we had. At the end we had only about seventy rifles, maybe fifty pistols, and a few hundred hunting rifles and muzzle loaders. Not a lot for fighting an army that brought cannons and machine guns and exploding shells against us.

Before noon on Saturday the English reached Batoche. I had placed riflemen on the right bank of the river below the cemetery where the river passes a long beach after flowing through a rapid. I knew that the *Northcote* would have to pass near the beach there, perhaps even try landing on it. I told my men to shoot the helmsman as the boat approached the rapid so it would drift out of control. On the other bank of the river I placed more fighting men, who could catch the boat in a crossfire.

I also gave the order to lower the ferry cable, to capsize the drifting steamer, but my men thought it was low enough. They fired on the wheel house and, as I had foreseen, the boat went adrift. As it was, the cable only knocked the smoke stacks off. A fire started on the deck, which the crew managed to put out in spite of my men firing on them. The *Northcote* was not put completely out of the battle, as I had hoped it would be, but dropped anchor where the river widens in front of my dead brother Isidore's house. I sent Michel Dumas and his men to prevent the English from repairing the boat. But they stopped before reaching Isidore's house and their mission was fruitless.

At the same time that we attacked the steam boat, Middleton's main column reached Caron's farm. Middleton tried to take Belle Prairie, and placed his machine gun so it could fire on Batoche. They were within a half mile of the church. I was about the same distance from them, watching on horseback. They fired the machine gun at me but the bullets all fell short.

We had rifle pits near the riverbank, the cemetery, and Emmanuel Champagne's house. They were a few feet deep and about seventy-five feet from one another, with two or three men in every one and trenches linking them together. I had about fifteen men in the rifle pits, with the rest scattered in the brush and small bushes. We had about one hundred and fifty men on the Batoche side of the river and about one hundred on the other bank, in addition to the squad of thirty that was harassing the steamboat.

I was not in favour of making the rifle pits at Batoche, though when we decided on them I made certain that they were very well made. This was not the open prairie where we could retreat and I knew what would happen. Our fighters would get down in them and feel secure there and forget to move. Then when the English advanced they would keep their heads down waiting for a sure shot, and when they looked up it would be too late.

Early in the fight, the English brought a cannon into action and fired on every building flying a Métis flag. We had a flag of the Virgin on Baker's house on the other side of the river, and a flag of Our Lord on the Council Building. This night the English pulled back. I had my men maintain an irregular fire on them as they made their camp and ate their meal. We continued to shoot throughout the night.

Old Norbert Sauvé was inside Baker's house. He was completely deaf. The English heated their cannon balls red hot before they fired them, and two or three times they set the house on fire. But each time the fire went out, as if by a miracle. In spite of the cannon fire and the flames on the outside of the house, Norbert Sauvé didn't realize that he was being fired on until a cannon ball went right through the house from end to end. Then he rushed outside and asked a young boy what was happening. The boy helped him flee to the woods.

The next morning, Middleton threw up earthworks so he could sleep more soundly. The English had control of the church and cemetery, and moved their machine gun to the small clearing at the top of the trail leading down into Batoche—to the left of the old trail and to the right of the new one.

I moved up on them with my men. As we crawled through the small aspens, I said, "First we must take the machine gun. Let me go on alone. I have already taken a shot in the head, and this time they might not miss. I will try to return their favour and put a bullet into the gunner's head. When I start shooting you try to draw his fire." I had almost reached a place where I could get off a clear shot when my men began firing. Branches began breaking all around me and I was completely pinned down. I withdrew before the artillery started shelling me and the English reinforcements arrived.

After the battle of Batoche we were defeated but not totally demoralized. I heard that Paul Chelet walked to the English camp and sought out the officer in charge of the machine gun. "Do you know how many Métis fighters that gun of yours killed?" he asked.

"No," said the Englishman. "But I'd like to."

"Just one," mocked Chelet, "and that was my horse."

Actually, the machine gun killed a little girl who strayed into the line of fire. It was a tragedy. She was just six or seven years old. When I was in New York City working for Buffalo Bill, a man came to see me and said, "I was the gunner. I fired the machine gun in front of the church. But that is over now, and even then I was only firing into the air to scare you."

I said, "Well, while you were trying to scare me, I was trying to put a bullet in your head. You are a lucky man to be here talking to me right now." He was an American from Montana and had fought for the U.S. Army during the Blackfoot war. I should have made an extra effort to kill him at Batoche.

At the end of the first day, the church stood on neutral ground, between our rifle pits and the English line. During the next three days the English could not move their lines. Nor did they kill a single one of my men. To draw their fire, we stuck up dummies as targets near the rifle pits and collected the bullets that fell by them. With English bullets filling the air around him, Riel walked unharmed along the front of the lines encouraging the Métis fighters.

At some point, Middleton rode to the church to speak to the priests. He despaired of ever defeating us, but Father Vegreville advised him that we did not have much ammunition and that he should try to make us use up our bullets.

The priests were openly ranged against us. They would no longer hear confessions—neither from the fighters nor from their wives and children. That was discouraging for the poor Métis. Before then, we were unenlightened. We had not completely believed Riel and the words of the priests had some truth in them. Since then, I see things more clearly. I think they were just like the Government: they lied to us from the beginning.

Each night the English soldiers returned to their camp. We often found little piles of bullets like deer pellets on the ground behind trees where they had stopped during the day to reload. It was our only source of new ammunition. We also found on many occasions cartridge bags containing forty gattling-gun cartridges, which were the same calibre as the repeating rifles we were using. That was when I also discovered that the English were using exploding grape shot. A simple bullet disables a man, but grape shot rips him open. Despite Riel's assertions, these men were no friends of ours. It is a crime against humanity that the Government used exploding shells against us.

The English began the final assault on the fourth day. The priests told them that we had no more ammunition, so they pushed in on all sides. When they routed our front line, they advanced all the way to Batoche's house without stopping. They charged in battalions, raining bullets on the rifle pits. My men held their fire, but there were so many English that they had no chance. Many were killed before they could escape from their pits.

I fought a rear guard for a half hour after the English entered the house of Batoche. Joseph Vandal Sr. and Joseph Vandal Jr. stayed with me, along with old Ouellette, Pierre Sansregret, David Tourond, and a young Sioux warrior. Daniel Ross was injured, and he called to me to come and drag him outdoors onto the battlefield.

"Are you hard hit?" I called.

"I won't last very long," he said, "but I want to fight on. Perhaps I can take a few more of them with me."

The English had occupied Batoche's house. There was a window on the second floor with a red curtain, and Captain French climbed up to fire on us. This is when Daniel Ross shot him. French was struck at the top of the staircase and rolled down. The English liked French and were furious that he had been killed. They bayoneted Ross as he lay wounded on the ground.

Joseph Vandal Sr. was wounded, both his arms broken, one in two places. He was seventy-five years old, but limped on toward the enemy. Finally he lost his balance and could not get back to his feet. "Uncle," I said as I helped him up, "you must escape."

"No," he said. "Leave me, nephew. I prefer to die here."

"Go! Go!" I screamed, but he would not go and told me again to leave him. So I obliged him and went back to fight from Batoche's basement.

This also was the time when my poor friend Damase Carrière died. When he fell with a wounded leg the English mistook him for Riel. They put a noose around his neck and dragged him behind a horse until he was dead.

My companions and I fought our way to the hilltop between Fisher's house and store, and held our position there. That was where old Ouellette was killed. I must say this: it was his courage that had sustained us all. Although he was ninety-three years old, he would not leave the battlefield. Several times I said, "Father, we must retire." And he answered, "Wait a minute. I only want to kill one more Englishman." "Okay," I said. "Let us die here." When he was shot, I thanked him and he sent me away. Then the young Sioux warrior fell with a bullet in his chest. He bled from the mouth, and we had to leave him too. Joseph Vandal Jr., Pierre Sansregret, and David Tourond were the only ones left with me.

"It is over," I said, "but we must continue to fight so our women and children can escape." Philippe Gariépuy, John Ross and his son, the son of Tom Anderson, Hilaire Paternotre, and my nephew Henry Smith joined us. We stalked the English in the half light, picking up bullets as we fought. At Emmanuel Champagne's house, I asked Hilaire Paternotre to look for a small barrel of black powder he knew about. He would not go. Henry Smith was very afraid, but when I asked if he would go he removed his shoes so he could run faster. He said, "Hold my rifle and my shoes, and I will get the powder." He gave his rifle to John Ross to carry.

We had not eaten since morning, and I remembered that one of the Sioux tipis had a lot of dried meat in it. I sent the others on toward my brother Edouard's house, then went and got an armful of dried meat. My companions found Madeleine and some other women. Near Edouard's, we found Riel and his wife and children.

"What are we going to do?" is what Riel said when he saw me.

"Die," I said to him. "Now we perish. With God's help you have been able to see into the future. You must have known when we took up arms that we would be defeated. So now they destroy us. What is the lesson I should take from this?"

Then I told him that I must go to our camp to find some blankets. I said that I would find a horse for him, so he could escape. He said that I exposed myself too much. I answered that the enemy was incapable of killing me—at this moment I felt like the angel of death himself, because for the first time I truly was without fear.

As I slipped off into the night, I heard Riel say to his wife, "I hope that God wants me to live, but I think that He must want me dead."

I crept to the tent where we had put the extra blankets. It was about fifty yards from a house the English soldiers had occupied. One of the soldiers stood framed in the door, and I shot him. Another came to look at the body and I weeded him out too. I carried two blankets and two quilts back to Madeleine, who gave them to Madame Riel and her children.

The others wanted to retreat farther away. I went back to the women's camp below Batoche in search of meat and flour. When I returned, Madeleine divided the food among the people who remained with us. Then I left a third time, to try and find more food and some horses.

Before I left, I said to Madeleine, "Wait for me here. If our enemies capture you, don't let them blame you for what I have done. Tell them that if they think of all the trouble I have caused them, then they might begin to understand what you have put up with all these years."

She said, "Shut up, husband. Go! Hurry back, and don't stop to play at killing any more Englishmen. There are women and children here who need you." But the soldiers had reached the camp and I had to return empty-handed. There were a lot of lost and confused women and children. Madeleine grew very worried for them. I led the people with me to another hiding place, then set off again to find some horses.

By then, night was on us. As I moved a white object attracted my eyes. I called twice and then, when I threatened to shoot, a weak voice said, "We are Métis." It was Madame Vandal, whose husband had died at my side some hours before. The old woman was paralyzed, but her daughter had carried her on her back until she fell exhausted in the snow.

A little farther away I heard some voices and hid. I was on the point of shooting when I recognized the voices of three young Métis fighters, who were searching for something to eat. They had found a sack of flour. At this moment, I heard some horses in the underbrush. We captured them—a Sioux pony and a Canadian stallion. I gave the pony to my young men and kept the stallion for myself. They gave me half their sack of flour.

The stallion was wild. He roared and reared as I led him toward the riverbank. I fell in again with my nephew Henry Smith and young John Ross. They had seen some more horses and helped me capture a mare. Then I stopped at a nearby house and took some dishes and utensils. I had tied the stallion outside, and his neighing attracted a bunch of mares to him. I heard them coming and froze. Thinking that they were soldiers, I was determined to kill some of them. When I realized that it was a bunch of horses, I released the stallion and set off with the mare. I found a goat, which I killed and brought with me, and a big loaf of bread that some English soldiers had dropped near the trail.

Madeleine was alone when I returned to her; the others had fled farther away from Batoche. I put her on the mare and we moved northeast. It was very cold, and I was only in my shirt-sleeves—at some time during the fight I had laid my coat down and forgotten it. Early the next morning we moved a little farther away, and I went on foot to find Riel.

From a high place I saw white flags flying from the roofs at Batoche. Everyone was surrendering their weapons. I met James Short, my brother-in-law, who had escaped on foot with my sister and another woman. Throughout the battle, he had fought like a tiger. Now he felt he could not hide with his horse. He told me where he had left it and as I searched for it, the three young Trottiers appeared looking for their mother. There were several free horses nearby, so I helped them capture one each before the soldiers got them all. I took one for myself, and learned from them that Napoléon Nault and the men on the west bank had given themselves up.

I returned to Madeleine. There were tracks everywhere, all leaving Batoche. We followed them, gathering together the scattered families we found. Near Montour Butte, about ten miles from Batoche, we found a group of women and children with some men protecting them. My foster-son Alexi was there. My brother Elie had killed a cow for them to eat and had cut some hay to cover them with. They looked like animals, but the women were very courageous and laughed at their situation. Most of the children had bare feet, so I made a kind of rawhide shoe for them to wear. We camped with them. In the morning, I gave one of my horses to Alexi and the other to the women for the children to ride. Madeleine and I then set off on foot for my father's house.

As we walked along the trail, we met three soldiers escorting some Indians. The Indians recognized me and told the soldiers who I was. They knew my reputation, so they sent one of the Indians to speak to me. When he drew near, I ordered him to stop.

"Are you afraid of me?" he asked.

"Certainly," I said. "Yesterday you fought at my side, but today you interpret for my enemies. If you come any closer I am afraid I will have to kill you. You tell these soldiers that I won't lay down my weapons. I will fight them forever, and the first one who makes a move toward my wife or me will die."

The soldiers kept their distance, particularly when the Indian told them what I had said. They left, with the intention undoubtedly of returning with reinforcements, and they were the last English soldiers to catch sight of me.

Now Madeleine began begging me to cross the line to Montana to avoid being captured. But I refused to escape before I knew what had happened to my unhappy friend. I left her at my father's house and searched again for Riel. As I travelled, I collected bullets the way a miser gathers coins. There were a few hundred riders searching for me, and I kept behind them the whole time.

This night I visited my father. I told him I had decided to spend the summer near Batoche, ambushing the soldiers and the police.

"I am very proud that you won't surrender," he said, "but this is a bad idea. If you remain here only to take vengeance on some soldiers, the world will call you an idiot and a criminal. You must escape to Montana. You are the only chief that the Métis have left. If you are killed or captured, your people will lose all hope."

"*Ai-caw-pow*, my father," I said, "your counsel was always good. I really want to follow it now, but I must find out what has happened to Riel. If I can not find him and persuade him to escape with me, then I will leave."

Then my father said, "Your brother-in-law Moïse Ouellette is here, and you must speak to him. He has a message from Middleton."

So I went to see Moïse, who told me that he had a letter for Riel and me. When I asked him what it said, he told me that it promised us justice if we surrendered. But Madeleine read it for me. She said that it didn't even mention me and said only: "I will accept the surrender of you and your Council, and let the Government Authorities decide your case."

"Moïse," I said. "You and Middleton can go right to hell. You have not even read this letter. The Government has clipped you like a lamb. It has unmanned you, and now you dance to its tune."

"Gabriel," Moïse answered, "Riel is a prophet, and it is fine for you to fight on heroically because you don't have any children of your own. You don't know what it is to see your children frightened and bewildered, their home destroyed; to know that everything you hoped for their future is gone. I *have* children, and I surrendered for their sake."

There was justice in his concern for my nieces and nephews, so I said, "You tell Middleton that Gabriel Dumont took to the woods. He has tried to destroy my house and my family and impoverish my nation, but I am still a man of means. I have one hundred and thirty bright coins to spend on his soldiers—ninety for le Petit and forty for my revolver. If he must count on anything in this life, he should count on my rifle and my sang-froid. Let his soldiers try to take me if they dare."

J. B. Parenteau gave me his best horse, which saved me and let me continue my search for Riel. Once I was sure that I had found him. I called out from a bluff, but there was no answer so I moved on. Nicholas Fageron said later that he had been with Riel and had heard me cry out. He had recognized my voice, but Riel thought it was an English trap and refused to answer me.

On the fourth day after the fall of Batoche, I met Moïse Ouellette again. He had lost his horse and asked me to give him one. I sent him to a family that had managed to take its horses before Middleton's army could steal them. As I left him Moïse said, "I gave the letter to Riel, and he went immediately to see the English general."

So the good Lord did not want me to see Riel again. I wanted to stop him surrendering, but he was very persuasive. Who knows? He might even have found a way to convert me to his point of view, and I might have surrendered with him.

At the end, Riel surrendered to save the rest of us. He offered himself as a sacrifice in our place. No one can deny that. He truly believed that the Government would be happy with his head and would leave the rest of us alone. How can someone not admire a man like that? Friends tell me that in jail he said,

"I know that I will be forgiven by God. I know, also, that both God and men will forgive Gabriel Dumont."

Joseph Delorme says that once Riel passed the door of his cell and whispered, "Do you know where Gabriel is?" When Delorme told him that I had crossed the line, he said, "Good. This is good for everyone. The Métis nation will survive. Depend on Gabriel. He will journey widely and be welcomed everywhere he goes. He will do great service for all of you. I am going to die, but Gabriel will ripen to a wise old age."

By May 16th, I was the only free warrior left, so I decided to take shelter in the United States. This night I camped with my brother Jean, who told me there were soldiers watching the house of our father. We sent my nephew Alexi to get some travelling food from my father and to tell Madeleine that I had decided to escape.

Always before I had known that I could return. Now I grew confused. How could I imagine existence without Madeleine? I might never see her again. Since the summer we married, we had always been together. Alexi returned with a message of love and a few fresh galettes—the only food my father could spare.

Next morning Jean brought me my charger, which he had found wandering free. He was the best horse in Batoche. Jean and some young men walked me to the edge of the grove I had hidden in. Then I mounted and set off. I had only gone about one hundred yards when I heard a shout and the drum of hooves behind me.

It was Michel Dumas. "Hello Mr. Dumont," he said as he rode up to me. "As you can see, I am still sympathetic to your cause. Would you like company for your long journey to Montana?"

"Hello, Mr. Rat," I said, smiling at him. "Have you any food with you?"

"Only some galettes," he said.

"Are you armed?" I asked.

"I lost my gun when the soldiers drove us from the rifle pits," he said.

"Oh well," I laughed. "I am sure we can count on le Petit to feed and protect the two of us." And so we set off by the Grace of God.

My heart was swollen with the storms of fifteen years and shattered by my failure. The weather turned clear and warm. Seized by emotion we crossed the prairie like falcons. The deepest solitude reigned in every small valley and on the crest of every hill. Images of the hunting caravans and the wars we had waged on the Indians surrounded me. Soon cities would spread over our trampled camping sites, and grain would sway where thousands of buffalo had bellowed at our appearance. When I said good-bye to my home, the prairie was an immense ocean scattered with islands of wood, sailed by clouds running with the wind. The land was resting for the long labour of invasion that lay ahead.

We journeyed in darkness, after the sun had set. Twice a day, through each soft evening and lucid dawn, our eyes and ears drank in the sacred dances of the prairie chickens. Their thrumming welcomed the King of Stars then bid Him farewell, the sound growing from the light itself. So intent were they on their dance that we could walk up and kill them with sticks. It was not a normal thing for Métis hunters to do, but in our extremity we thanked them for their gift of life.

At Lizard Mountain, about ten miles south of Batoche, we turned southeast toward Last Mountain Lake. We kept wide of Saskatoon, crossed the Qu'Appelle in the Vermilion Hills, and disappeared deep into the Mauvais Bois. My head wound troubled me. Sometimes I fell to the earth unconscious. Every small Indian and Métis camp fed us and offered sympathy. My uncle Jean welcomed us to the Cypress Hills, although the police had two posts established near his home, one at Fort Walsh and another on the Milk River. After eleven days on the march, we crossed finally into Montana.

Throughout this journey I had felt blessed and protected, and never stopped saying to the sacred Virgin, "You are my mother! Lead me." But I also put faith in my rifle. We didn't see a single police patrol, which was, I think, partly because they respected what le Petit would do to them if they found me. My first thought on crossing the line was to kneel and say the rosary.

Soon after we crossed the border, a cavalry patrol arrested us. The sergeant in charge was a Canadian who took us to Fort Assiniboine. He walked us down a long passageway and showed us to a cell.

Dumas was furious. "Relax, Mr. Rat," I said. "At least we will not have to sleep outside tonight. These beds will do very nicely."

However, a few moments later the sergeant returned and apologized to us. His officer had insisted that we move to a better room. They took us to a larger cell, without bars and with a cavalry officer of our own to serve us and make new apologies for the way we were treated. Finally the commander of the fort visited us. He spoke French and said that he had telegraphed the Government of the United States about our case. Three more days and we were released to travel freely where we wanted.

For me, Montana was not the end of our resistance. Madeleine's brother, David Wilkie, had a house at Spring Creek, near Lewiston. With it as a base, Dumas and I worked to raise money. Though I had been incapable of protecting Riel at Batoche, I refused to surrender him to death. I set about to rescue him from the hands of our enemies. More refugees arrived every day, and the people of Montana saw first-hand the injustices and indignities we suffered. Before long, my brothers Edouard and Jean joined me, bringing our brother-in-law Baptiste Parenteau with them.

It was good they arrived. By then Michel Dumas was drinking away our money and condemning every part of our rebellion except the role he had played. People began to stop offering us support. Our plans were not safe with him.

One night I dragged him from a bar. "Rat," I said, "your part in this affair is over. Your sympathies are apparent. I did not lead my nation to war for this. We will have nothing more to do with you. You won't squander any more of our money. Don't ask for a place among us again." I don't regret doing that to him, and he has never forgiven me. He slipped away to join Buffalo Bill's Wild West Show, where his only responsibilities were to himself.

My brothers and I rode hard between Lewiston and the Métis camps. Finally we had horses and supplies placed all the way to Regina. But the police got word of our plans. They tripled their guards until they had a ring of guards around Riel. There was no way we could reach him. Again he had placed his faith in me. Again I had failed him.

GEORGE WOODCOCK, *interpreter*

While Dumont was organizing the plot to rescue Riel, Madeleine travelled south from Saskatchewan to join him. She had missed him and had persuaded Patrice Fleury, who was her sister's husband, to accompany her and Annie to Lewiston. She brought the news that Gabriel's father had died.

After she joined him at Lewiston, Gabriel grew aware of her unaccustomed lack of energy, of her drawn features, and of the strange alternations of depression and elation in her behavior; but there were other things dragging at his attention. In the spring of 1886 Madeleine fell from a buggy. No bones were broken, but she never recovered and died soon afterward. Some said it was from her injuries, and others from the consumption that only a few weeks earlier had claimed Riel's young wife.

PATRICE FLEURY, *defeated Métis fighter*

Madeleine Dumont was my wife's sister. After Gabriel fled, she and Annie stayed with us, but Madeleine got very bored just sitting around, and finally I agreed to take her to Montana to be with her husband. By now Tom McKay had a great deal of influence with the English, so I told him what I planned to do.

"Don't do it," he said.

"Why?" I asked.

"Patrice," he said. "If you go you will be arrested. Father André and Father Fourmond and I have already gone to a lot of trouble to keep you out of prison. Don't waste what we have done for you."

"Tom," I said, "I have to go. Since the war my wealth is gone. It is all I can do to keep my own family alive. I can not support two more people."

So Tom McKay got me a pass from the English and I sold a horse and a cow to raise money for the trip. The Dumonts were scattered to the winds. On the way south we met Eduoard's wife and I lent her a horse to get to Fort Assiniboine to be with her husband. All the way we found fighters who had escaped, most of them on their way into exile.

It took us several days. We had some trouble with some Blackfoot Indians near the border until they realized that we were Métis. But then they fed us and helped us on our way. Gabriel was very glad to see Madeleine, and I felt he had been thinking that it was possible that they might never meet again. Sadly, she did not live long after I took her down there. I heard that she fell out of a buggy and was so badly injured that she died. Madeleine was a fine woman, and we all miss her very much. What my children learned of reading they learned from her.

5

Jesus! Mary! Joseph! Pray for us.
Regina Prison, 6 July 1885

To CAPTAIN R.B. DEAN, Commanding Officer at Regina.
To HIS HONOUR EDGAR DEWDNEY, Lieutenant Governor of
the Territories of the North-West.
To THE VERY HONOURABLE SIR JOHN A. MACDONALD,
Prime Minister of the Dominion of Canada.

Captain; Your Honour; Mister Prime Minister:
Many years before confederation, Mister Gabriel Dumont
was at the head of a Métis council in the North-West. That
council was called the Council of Prairie Law. Permit me to
speak about it—I don't have the slightest intention of making
any unpleasant allusion. Though all the Indian Chiefs, even
the most unimportant, were acknowledged in one way or
another by the Government, Mister Gabriel Dumont was
completely ignored. That still offends his soul. I could see that
when he came to seek me last year in Montana.

But this year, when his petitions did not get attention;
when schemers plotted war against him and his people; when,
while fighting that war, he lost more close relatives than
anyone else; when his brother Isidore was killed at his side;
when he himself was wounded and drenched with his own
blood; when his Councillor of Councillors, who he himself
nominated and who was elected on his recommendation, is
imprisoned, chained; when instead of the promised honest
trial the Government prevents me from communicating with
my attorneys and deprives them of the simplest means of
providing for my defense—I leave you to imagine what takes
place in the heart and mind of Mister Dumont. His outrage
should be easy to imagine.

My fate occupies him. He probably hears that I am treated as a murderer, that I am kept in a very small cell. He lived with me, and I with him, for several months. He knows how indispensable air, exercise, and proper food are for my health. He might conclude that you are trying to kill me through over-strict captivity.

Furthermore, the newspapers' stories could lead him to understand that you are going to try me simply for form's sake; that you wish to condemn me at any price; that a guilty verdict already hovers over me.

I am in all this trouble as a result of having agreed to come to assist him in writing the petitions which he had to make. I know him. He will believe himself obliged to come to my rescue, to assist his friend, if there is a way.

O my pen! Be persuasive. The men you address are very distinguished. Express my meanings without annoying them. When my thoughts are bleak or painful, take care. Those who read what you write truly deserve that, in return for their attention, you are respectful and considerate toward their intelligence.

My kinsman Mister Gabriel Dumont will seek, I am absolutely certain, to forge a relationship with sympathetic people in Montana, particularly in the mines, which are numerous and considerable in that territory.

The miners are, generally speaking, people of great boldness. They are always well armed and are fine marksmen. Their lack of concern for their lives has become proverbial. They don't often make their fortunes in the mines. And when a diversion or a surprise tumbles into their life, there are many among them who heed its invitation. Mister Dumont's brilliant leadership as a man of war in the Saskatchewan could not fail to give him prestige in their eyes.

I don't say that he *will* attack the North-West; but supposing that he might, his forays could be very serious. Mister Gabriel Dumont has a genius for military operations. He knows the North-West like the palm of his hand. And might not the Americans take the opportunity, by leaving him alone, of rendering to Canada and Britain what many of them believe they suffered when Sitting Bull retreated to this side of the line?

However, let us assume that Mister Dumont stays peaceful. Even in that case, I do not think he will remain idle.

He is going to try communicating with the Fenians, and, through their mediation in the United States, with other nationalities, with the goal of fashioning a league capable of backing the Métis, sooner or later, in the assertion of their rights on the North-West.

He will address Societies known for their hostility towards Canada. He will tell them simply that the Canadian Government is required, by testimony of the treaty, to grant the Métis of the North-West one-seventh of the territory for the extinction of their Indian title to the land; that this principle was inaugurated in Manitoba where—on an area of almost 9,500,000 acres—the Dominion set aside 1,400,000 acres for them. He will add that the Canadian Government doesn't wish to keep its bargain with the Métis of the North-West; that since the stipulations for the entrance of this great Territory into the Confederacy are not being followed, there is no constitutional union between the North-West and Canada.

Mister Dumont secretly prepares to declare his country free.

Since my status as an American citizen bestows on his declaration a reason for its originating from the United States, he will probably assume my name to make it. He will present the appeal for help as coming more from me than from him. For my kinsman, Mister Gabriel Dumont, knows very well that by having a citizen address his fellows he can more certainly succeed in gaining American sympathies.

It is in this way that the means to action become popular.

He will enter into negotiations with Irish, French-Canadian, Italian, Polish, and Jewish organizations. He will offer to cede to each of these nationalities enough land to create a province of their own in the North-West. They, in return, will guarantee him numerous well-supplied colonists. These covenants, enacted by a notary public or before some court of the United States, will enjoy a proper air of legality to give them vogue.

In the United States, judicial offices are elective. One might even say that in the Irish counties they are entirely under the Irish influence. The country is full of magistrates who would take pleasure in preparing contracts of this kind.

Mister Gabriel Dumont, and all those whom his offer might influence, will say: "Riel, at the head of the Métis, treated with Canada in 1870. His treaty is valid on the point of being the constitution of Manitoba. However, in contravention of that treaty he was hunted, banished from his country.

"Once again at the head of the Métis, and more in their confidence than ever, today that same Riel is now an American citizen. So he can treat for the North-West with the American Government, and his treaty will be valid."

They will perhaps proclaim that, by the nature of the Indian title to the land, when I became an American I took my Métis right with me to the United States; and that, with regard to my native blood, I am to the American Republic a little like an Indian at the head of his tribe, with his territory under the jurisdiction of the Government in Washington; that my naturalization papers place the international boundary in question; and that Americans can lawfully spread into the North-West, whether out of Dakota or Montana.

Mister Gabriel Dumont is devoted to me, with a devotion, thanks to God, difficult to surpass. He would wish that I be recognized as the leader of the Métis in all of British North America. He himself would lead the Métis of the North-West on this side of and beyond the Rocky Mountains, as far as the Sea. His position is that the Métis of Manitoba obtained one-seventh of the lands of that province: that the Métis of British Columbia are also entitled to their seventh of the lands, since their title is absolutely the same.

With regard to British Columbia, the plan is to offer shares of it to Belgian, Bavarian, Danish, Swedish, and Norwegian organizations, on the condition of their leaving one-seventh of the land for the Métis after they secure it.

As for the eastern Canadian provinces, a lot of Métis there live scorned as Indians. Their villages are impoverished. Their Indian title to the land is, however, as absolute as the Indian title of the Métis of Manitoba. They will one day have their seventh of the land or an adequate income from the Germans of the United States, who will be invited to invade the two Canadas and the Maritime provinces. If that undertaking were to be crowned with success, the Germans' compensation would be to occupy the regions of Lake Superior and Lake Huron from the American border as far as the coast of the Northern Sea; and therein to establish a Germany for them-selves in the New World.

Mister Gabriel Dumont is not learned, but he has a fine intellect. He cut truly into his mind the names of the nation-alities that are important to him. He can count those names on six fingers. One-seventh of the territory for the Métis is not a difficult notion to retain. The offers he has to present are well thought through.

He may even have with him, on paper, a synoptic chart of the proposal. He will have only to place it in the hands of the Irish organizations. Mister Dumont has confidence in the Irish as agitators of great force. It is through their intervention that he wishes to set the other nationalities in motion.

He is not unaware that the Jews are rich; that they suffer bitterly by being without a homeland; and that if he could assist them to leave one for their children, they would set to work with an extraordinary zeal. It is consequently with the Jews, on the one hand, and the Irish, on the other, that Mister Gabriel Dumont hopes to launch, in the United States, the foundations of a grand and attractive league.

Gentlemen, whether or not you choose to regard this letter as a friendly warning, as I hope you will, rest assured that although you have me, you will never capture Mister Gabriel Dumont. He is a very determined man, in whom our cause lives on. Therefore, I humbly suggest that your best policy may be to convince public opinion that I will have a full and open trial; and that "Fair Play" is going to be accorded to all the prisoners of war.

If, by special good fortune, Mister Gabriel Dumont has not made his overtures on the other side of the line, those favourable reports with respect to me and the other Métis will have, I am confident, a great effect on him; and could keep him calm and waiting with some hope.

If, on the other hand, he is already in contact with the Irish organizations, the "Land League," for example, it is very probable that the French-Canadian and Jewish organizations are also aware of his offers and in possession of his program.

In that case, your treatment of your prisoners must be calculated in such a way as to influence as directly as possible the Irish, the French-Canadians, and the Jews themselves.

You have only to establish in public opinion the certainty that we are all truly going to have "Fair Play."

If I have "Fair Play" in Court—with God's help—I will soon be cleared. Immediately upon gaining my liberty, I will write to Mister Gabriel Dumont. If I recommend it to him, he will certainly return to this side of the line, nobly, to submit himself for his trial.

I have the honour,
Captain, Governor,
Mister Prime Minister,
of Being,
Very respectfully yours,
LOUIS RIEL

6

Hate is not the enemy of Love. They stand together in the battle against fear and loneliness. The only real question is: How long can we battle against those currents? How long can we beat against that terrible water, with nothing solid to keep us afloat?

Riel died a saint and a martyr. He took nothing for himself and gave his life for his nation. He was persecuted and betrayed. He got a mock trial. His persecutors washed their hands and offered him to his executioners. And what were the charges against him? That he had resisted a Government. That he had prophesied and blasphemed! But the indignant explosion that followed his execution was an exhibition of conscience. His exaltation proves the justice of our cause. His God gave the Métis people more than the priests' God ever offered. Dignity is always more satisfying than blind obedience. The morning Riel walked through the sunlight to the scaffold, I watched the light glitter on the hoar frost. The prairie was a sea sown with diamonds, a raging prairie fire. Then a cloud passed over and snapped out the light.

About Buffalo Bill and his Wild West Show, I don't have much to say. A man once showed me a newspaper that said Buffalo Bill had introduced me to the King and Queen of England. The photograph in the paper was of Michel Dumas. Maxime Lépine, brother of Riel's old general Ambroise Lépine, was with him. They had accompanied the Wild West Show to Europe, but Buffalo Bill soon sent them on their way because they were always drunk. They stayed with him until they got here, to Paris. And after they left Buffalo Bill they roamed the streets of

Paris, eventually knocking on the door of the Canadian Consulate where Dumas introduced himself as me. The mayor of the Commune of Neuilly had heard that I was in Paris and wanted to meet me. He himself had been a general, and showed great interest in Dumas. It was owing to his intercession that the Rat returned to Canada as Gabriel Dumont. But now that I am here myself in Paris you Parisians can judge for yourselves the differences between Dumas and me.

While I was with the Wild West Show in New York City, I met Crozier for the last time. He seemed beaten and devastated, but was pleasant enough to me, not spiteful. His career as a police officer had died on the battlefield at Duck Lake, but he brought me good news. He said that the Canadian Government would offer amnesty to all the Métis fighters who had escaped to the United States, so I would be able to return to the Saskatchewan.

Since the rebellion I have continued to pursue the goals that Riel laid out for us. But the French in the United States and Canada don't like what I tell them about their priests, so here I am in Paris looking for support. I am a simple man, but I do know that what men say and what they do are very different things. I have been here nearly one year already, have never left this city; and how lonely I find the lives you lead. I have listened to and spoken with many of your chiefs and politicians, and always I say this to them: great men may believe that the ideals they hold are true for all mankind, but every private man learns to embrace struggle, bitterness, and small triumphs and humiliations as his truths. Chiefs must lead, but they must also follow. They must feel for the true wishes and needs of their people, then try to satisfy them. Otherwise their nations will suffer for their leaders' pride and conduct. Riel knew this.

Two years ago I visited the Métis hunting camps in Dakota. At one place I camped with some hunters I knew, but slept in a tent of my own. During the night a knife blow above my left ear awakened me. I bounded to my feet, throwing off my attacker. Why did he want to kill me? As I fought him off I asked, "Why are you attacking me?" I was not angry, I was surprised. Why was a man I had never seen before trying to kill me?

He was a Hercules and armed like a meat cutter. He stabbed me many times in the back before I pinned him finally with a knee on his shoulders and beat his hands away. I stuffed my right hand down his throat, and he choked. I seized his knife in my left hand; it sliced deep into my fingers. My neighbours in the nearby tents woke up to the noise, and when they saw me choking my enemy they pulled me off him and he fled.

I think he was after the $5,000 reward that the Canadian Government still has on my head, because although we are amnestied the Government does not want me to lecture and tell the true history of our rebellion.

This assassin deserved my respect, and I wish he was here now. He knew his mind and cut right to the meat. He very nearly killed me. He slashed me twice across my stomach, once on the left side just below my ribs, and once a bit lower, under the navel. He was one of us, and I was very lucky he didn't puncture my abdomen. Each wound was four or five inches long, wide gashes that flowed blood in rivers... They left tremendous scars that make a great show on my belly...

Here is my catalogue of scars: a permanent bruise from the Year of the Great Peace; the long furrow the bullet plowed at Duck Lake; an assassin's dark slashes across my belly and below my ear; the hole in my heart where Madeleine lived. These moments, written hard on my body, inflame my memories. Yet they rest hidden and mysterious, though evident to the touch, burning with the bright pain of my losses. And there are others too; deeper, less visible. Scars and cities are lonely places; lonelier than the wind rattling a serpent's abandoned skin.

This story has seen years in the telling. I suspect it was difficult for you to feel our suffering? Did you enjoy the violence of our tragedy? Life does not easily surrender its mysteries. Although not noble or good like Riel, I am not a savage. So thank you for your visits, Monsieur Demanche. I think I've safely told you all you wanted to hear. Good day to you.

AUTHOR'S AFTERWORD

ONE LIBERATING DIFFERENCE between history and fiction lies in the fact that fiction can address unrecorded, and often unrecordable, aspects of living. Though I have tried not to take too many liberties, fiction has allowed me to explore Gabriel's story by bridging gaps in the documentary record and attempting to excavate some of his interior life. Many writers have portrayed Gabriel Dumont as an unlettered man, but that view can be debated, and there is in fact a remarkably extensive documentary record of his activities. That record, conjoined to first-person commentaries recorded by his family, friends, associates, and enemies—both during the period encompassed by this narrative and in the years from the disaster of 1885 until his death in 1906—has enabled me to explore his life as I imagine it was lived on the central plains during the last half of the nineteenth and first decade of the twentieth centuries.

Throughout this book I have attempted to cling with some tenacity to the historical documentation, and made the effort in every case to do my own translations from the French, however rough those efforts may have been. Though I probably can't reveal the wellsprings of my historical vision, I do want to point interested readers toward what I consider to be the essential historical records and sources. Furthermore, there are some excellent secondary sources that I can recommend, with the caveat that I may not agree with the positions the authors took but do admire the scholarship they display.

No one can think about Gabriel Dumont without first reading George Woodcock's fine biography *Gabriel Dumont: The Métis Chief and His Lost World*. However, Gabriel's own words must remain the foundation for any original examination of his life, and Woodcock did not footnote his book or provide a bibliography for it.

The outstanding historian of the period is George F. Stanley: any work by him demands thoughtful and sustained attention. In an article entitled "Gabriel Dumont's Account of the North West Rebellion" (*Canadian Historical Review*, no. 30 (1949): 249–69), Stanley was the first to translate and present Gabriel's own words in English. His source was Adolphe Ouimet's edited transcription of B.A.T. Montigny's interview with Gabriel, which took place in December of 1888 and was published as part of *La Vérité sur la question Métisse* (Montreal, 1889). (My own translation of that material was superseded in part by an extraordinary one done of some of the ancillary text by Carole Beaulieu.)

Remarkably, no one published a translation of Gabriel's other memoir until 1993, when Michael Barnholden produced *Gabriel Dumont Speaks* (Vancouver: Talonbooks), although a good translation did exist in the Provincial Archives of Manitoba (PAM MG10, F1, Box 12). It is in this other memoir, originally transcribed in 1903, that Gabriel mentions that he stayed in Paris for a year; it also appears to be the foundation for Sandra Lynn McKee's unashamedly pulpy and delightful *Gabriel Dumont: Indian Fighter* (Calgary: Frontier Publishing Ltd., 1973). Taken together, Gabriel's memoirs clearly represent his version of the events leading up to the catastrophe at Batoche.

Glimpses of Gabriel's larger life begin to emerge in the second memoir and in the ancillary material surrounding the first one as it appears in *La Vérité sur la question Métisse.* To amplify on those flashes I turned first to various archival sources— particularly to a group of interviews collected by A.H. de Trémaudan (PAM MG10, F1, Box 12); to the "Memoire de Ph.

Garnot" (PAA, 84.400/733); and to Edward Blake's report on and associated letters regarding the St. Laurent incident (NAC CO42, Vol. 737, reel B573; and RG18, Vol. 6, dossier 333/1875). Among the published sources, I relied on both John Kerr's own "Gabriel Dumont: A Personal Memory" (*Dalhousie Review*, no. 15, April 1935/January 1936: 53–59) and Constance Kerr Sissons's *John Kerr* (Toronto: Oxford, 1946). Also notable were W.F. Butler's *The Great Lone Land* (Edmonton: Hurtig, 1968); Guillaume Charette's *Vanishing Spaces: Memoirs of Louis Goulet* (R. Ellenwood, tr.; Winnipeg: Editions Bois-Brûlés, 1976); Hugh A. Dempsey's *Big Bear: The End of Freedom* (Lincoln: University of Nebraska, 1986); Joseph Kinsey Howard's *Strange Empire: The Story of Louis Riel* (Toronto: Swan, 1965); Eric Nicol's *The Astounding Long-Lost Letters of Dickens of the Mounted* (Toronto: McClelland and Stewart Inc., 1989); *The Collected Writings of Louis Riel* (G.F.G. Stanley et al., eds. 5 vols. Edmonton: University of Alberta Press, 1985); and Mary Weekes' account of Norbert Welsh's fascinating and compulsively self-involved memoirs, *The Last Buffalo Hunter* (New York: Thomas Nelson and Sons, 1939). Secondary sources that I found particularly rewarding included Bob Beal and Rod Macleod's *Prairie Fire: The 1885 North-West Rebellion* (Edmonton: Hurtig, 1984), and Thomas Flanagan's two books: *Louis "David" Riel: Prophet of the New World* (Toronto: University of Toronto Press, 1979) and *Riel and the Rebellion: 1885 Reconsidered* (Saskatoon: Western Producer Prairie Books, 1983). The musical notation is from Barbara Cass-Beggs's *Seven Métis Songs of Saskatchewan* (Don Mills, Ontario: BMI Canada Limited, 1967); the sketch of Gabriel's homestead appeared in the Toronto *Mail* on 29 May 1885; and the sketch of the rifle pit was, I think, done at Batoche by Captain H. de H. Haig for the *Illustrated London News* (I found it on the internet and have not yet been able to establish a hard attribution for it).

I accept responsibility for every contortion that was forced on the documentary evidence, and only hope that I have not offended the people who matter.

—JORDAN ZINOVICH, 1999